THE TWO STREETS

HIABU HASSEBU

SCRIPTOR HOUSE
THE EPITOME OF GREATNESS

ACKNOWLEDGMENTS.

The Two Street, would not have been possible, without my moral insistence. I'm grateful, to the devoted, my agent Alex Smith, who made my book to be optioned, by Hollywood. My thanks, to all members of Scriptor House, whom I met, via telephone or other means. Special, and heart filled, of "Thank you", reach to my son, Sibhat, who helped me in every dimension of my life.

PROLOGUE

It must have been close to four o'clock in the afternoon and I was making ready all my bags, before I was to fly to Hollywood, to pitch my book, the next day. Getting mentally tired of packing, I sat on a chair, in front of my laptop. I clicked to the Facebook page. Yohannes Ferdinando, was in line. He greets me by texting "Hi" on my private box.
Suddenly, he connects with me, via a phone.
"Are you planning to publish another book" he asks.
"writing's my hobby" I respond.
"I'm proud of you, Hiabu", he says.
"If the horses are not available to pull the cart, the donkeys are ready", I respond.
"Really, I'm surprised about you", he repeats, feeling happy.
"Nothing to be surprised about", I say.
"I'm just using the God given talent only" I conclude.

My life's settled into a routine, of going to work for six days a week and staying in front of the computer for several hours. The reality of being an author, if it was not from my mental tenacity, it wouldn't be a reality.

It's the beginning of summer 2010, July 4, a special and historical day, for all Americans. All Keren High School association group, are gathered in DC area, in Alexandria, Hilton hotel. Despite my loneliness I decided to join the event. Bereket Desta, as he sees me, stepping towards the main entrance gate of the hotel, he greets me with a cultural greetings, "Selamat". "I read your second book "Padre" in one day", he says. "Good, at least I got a moral complement", I respond.

This time, the I say, "Let me go novel", when deciding to recount, the true story of my life, living in Garrison neighborhood. The street's particular, bearing its unique character of my life adventure. The contents of my story, in its entirety, is a full fact of truth, right now happening as I type. The names on the story, are selected randomly. I'm trying to make an issue, to everything, that has fallen in my eyes.

* * * * * * * *

The Two Streets

THIS'S GARRISON.

This's Garrison Blvd. a testing spot situated on the western side of Baltimore city. If it can ever be described, by an immigrant mind, it's a place where cowardice of the neighborhood is tested; where cursing is practically recited on the street; where honesty and greed are in confrontational mood; where one don't know, who's friend or enemy.

Is very rear to hear the word "Thank you". Respect is out of the area. To be polite is seen as weakness. The word "Yo" is a common word, a dominant expression. The new generation of the neighborhood, they communicate without actually communicating. Good manner is not its location. Forged money circulates, almost on a daily bases. Heavy and monotonous sounds of Hip-hop songs pound and dominate the street. As one raises his voice to curse, the other is forced to curse. Argument is a normal process; fighting's a spectacle to be viewed; really it's a live movie, not pitched to the Hollywood film producers.

For whatever might be, life in Garrison street, spins, around the same experience, selling drugs. I stand there, immersed in a deep thought. An aura of memories come to my mind. The old, when I was back home and the new, living as an immigrant in Garrison neighborhood. The neighborhood residents, they call me by the name Mike. I've seen every kind of crime being committed, right in front of my eyes. I feel bad of one social class of blacks killing each other.

Garrison's a terrible street, it had always been like that, for more than fifty years. It takes the boys and girls away, from their schools, where they should be and hire them to sell drugs. They give them guns and tell them to kill each other. There's much evil, running loose on the street.

Now let me introduce my readers, the way I like to. I compare two streets, two life experience in two continents. My mind continuously, tries to connect the two streets of Keren and the famous Garrison street. I don't follow any organized chronology and in my style of composing it, it's neither as it comes in my mind. My expectations, are running high and optimistic.

* * * * * * * * *

Grandma, (in her mid-seventies) is at home in her own Villa. That morning she wakes up early from her sleep. The dog wakes her up, by gently barking, patiently sitting near the couch, with his paws crossed gracefully. Goes down from her bed, still with her night wear, stepping towards the dog. With the dog food in a bowl, in her hands, steps towards the dog. Bows down to the floor, as a bright light from top, shines on the ceramic floor.

Looks at the dog, murmurs like talking to it.
"It's good to have an animal as a companion".... "They give your days a purpose, to feed and take care of them", she says letting out a long and a deep breath. She blinks at the dog, smiling weakly. "Tomik", she shouts gently, by calling the dog by its name. The dog, whines and wiggles its tail. Sits besides Grandma on the couch, while she watches TV.

Her eyes widely open, after she becomes tired of watching the TV, remotely she puts it off. Instantly, her mind started to revolt.
"I need a break", she sighs.
"I can't stop my Grandson from what he is doing."
Walks out to the veranda stepping slowly. She sits on a coach, her view being on the green grass.
"Why he doesn't give himself a brake?" she murmurs, just thinking about her grandson weird life.
"I myself feel weak".... "No energy to confront my grandson.

Walks real slow, through the compound of the villa, very worried and concerned, about the daily crimes reports, broadcast by the local TV. Gets tired from the walk and steps up the stairs, with the help of her cane. As she reaches the last step of the stairs, breaths deeply and sits on the wooden couch. Suddenly, turns her face towards Liberty Height street. The street's full a folk, kids playing soccer on the street.
"I'm tired of all this noises." she repeats. Her mind no more can entertain it. The silent street it used to be, now she can't bare it.

As she's curled tight onto the coach, a yellow ball rolls a few feet, in her yard. A little Boy 11, runs across the street, to recover it. When he sees Grandma sitting under the veranda, he stops dead.
"Really I am in trouble." he says, his heart beating fast.
Runs and snatch it up. Turns and dashes off like he scared, she gone get him. Grandma, turns and looks straight at the kid, as he is jumping out over the wall.
"Poor kid! I hope he never joins the awful street of Garrison." she expresses, remembering the time of her youth age, living in

the neighborhood.
"In my life I have seen good and bad". She says, struggling walking back inside.

WITH THE RUMBLING PARTNER.

Lee pulls out from his right pocket, an already loaded marijuana cigar, trying to light it, raising his dark eyeglass facing towards the full moon. Puffing his cigar, gazes at Nicky, as she is busy arranging her braided hair. "What a beautiful moon?" he says, looking sideway to Nicky.
She sighs, gazing at her face, in front of the right mirror, still brushing and wiping her face with makeups, without saying a single word.
"Am I alone to enjoy this natural scenario?" ... "No comment?" he says, getting angry for her silence.
Nicky, bites her lips, giving him a long sober look.
"Good for you!"... "But I wonder if you are really admiring it through your natural eyes."
He frowns at her.
Bows towards the recorder, and starts to browse for some hiphop music.
"What do you mean by that? I'm sort confused." He sighs.
She stretches both her hands on her thigh, staring at her tiny decorated finger nails.
"You see when one is intoxicated, the natural way of admiring the nature, loses its sense."

Nicky, after staying long with Lee, inside the car, she manages to get herself out and sneaks inside a Mini-beauty shop. Mary, the owner from Senegal, is doing her daily job, braiding another female customer. As she sees Nicky stepping towards her, raises up from the sofa and greets her. "Darling nice to see you again." "By the way, yesterday you were here, did you come for unfulfilled services?" she asks, Nicky, walks quietly, towards the long chair and sits down, looking her face towards the big mirror.
"No. Just to take a break for my own reasons."

Mary, walks backward to serve her customer, looking at Nicky side way. "You know, if everything is OKAY with you, as our wise people say "don't ask again"."

Lee, remains restlessly in his car seat, waiting for Nicky to come out of the store, listening in a high volume, the Hiphop music. He struggles in his mind, trying to look cool, despite the secret of his relationship with Nicky, as his younger sister.
"I am getting a little tired of playing this particular Issue of the secret of my relationship with Nicky."

Honks three four times, as he is still waiting Nicky, sitting inside his car, smoking his cigar. As she sees him, she waves her hand. Runs towards him, where he is waiting her and enters the car. Few seconds later, both start to argue in a low voice. He forwards a rude question, she never expected. "Whom were you talking with?"
Nicky, sits at the age of the car seat, tilting towards Lee 90 degree, as though she is giving him a cheek kiss.
"With Mary, my hair braider."… "Anyway, no male involved to make you jealous."
He raises his eyebrow up and down.
"Not worried about that at all?"… "But-"
She breathes in and then out, pondering to the truth of her statement, shaking her head impatiently.
"But what?"
He sits back, by reclining the driver seat downward, as he shrugs looking embarrassed. "Let the truth remain for tomorrow."… "One thing at a time."
Nicky, looks at his face straight, with her big and clear eyes, in a feeling of sadness.
"Not my business to inquire about tomorrow's either."… "UN accepted interrogation, I refuse to reply." She tries to stay angry, at the same time as she smiles.
"Well, then I will tell you the truth, when due time."

Hiabu Hassebu
THE STRUGGLE OF GRANDMA.

It's mid-summer. Exactly, at 11:30 the big bell of All The Saints church, begin to ring loud. The service starts at midday sharp. Grandma, gets ready herself, to go to Church, wearing her white dress and a decorated hat. Before she leaves, she steps towards the big mirror, to check her vestment stand. She nods and walks towards her car. The dog starts to bark, in a low tone. She stares at the dog and glances back her way stepping towards the parked car.

She gets there early, parking at the parking lot, already full of cars. After the service is finished all the congregant step out through the main door entrance. Outside the stairs the Pastor is standing at the front door, to greet all congregant. Grandma, sneaks through the crowd, to greet the pastor. She looks up at Pastor, as her face is turned to brown, gazing in a weak smile, her eyes half closed. The Pastor, steps close to her, putting his hand over her, to bless her as she bows her head down.
"I imagine you are wondering about something, that I am reading from your mind."
Grandma Nods.
"I'm sorry." he says cheerfully glancing at her.
Grandma, says nothing.
Then her voice trailed off.
He looks at her coldly.
Feeling desperate, Grandma, she voices, "I have to straighten up Lee's life."... "Things can't work like that."... "Nothing is easy with this kind of life."... I'm sick and tired, simply passing off my joy and happiness, for somebody else's."
"I feel you!" he responds, one more blessing her with a greetings.

Grandma, walks slowly down the stairs and steps along a paved sidewalk path, glancing at her watch and striding towards her car. In the middle of the sidewalk, suddenly, she stops and looks towards the old church, making a sign of the cross. Enters into her old white Cadillac and starts the engine. She drives towards home, sitting speechless, thinking of the worst thing could happen, if she openly interacts with Lee her grandson. Looks straight at the front mirror, straightening her big white hat left and right.
"I wish he understands all my sacrifices.

* * * * * * * * * * * *

Old Gothic style Villa, facing east of Liberty High street, is the house of Grandma.

In front of the Villa, there is flower bed area surrounded by green grass, in the middle with the statues of Mary.

Parks her car in front of the villa; the dog barks non-stop. Trying to calm the dog, she slowly steps towards the dog. The dog greets her by wiggling its tail, standing straight up, like trying to reach her upper body.

Lee's sitting on a wooden chair, outside the veranda, holding on his right hand, a plastic water bottle and on his left, wiping his sweat with a handkerchief. Looks pale, as he entertains, with his early morning of marijuana. He gently pats, a place over his heart.
"I feel safe living with my Grandma, despite her fucking control over me."
He's having his last marijuana puff, as his Grandma steps in the house, through the main door. Suddenly, he throws his cigar to the garden. Knowing that, there is no chance of being relieved, from the usual conversation, he instead of confronting his Grandma, moves abruptly, along the street pavement.
"Here she comes, here we go!"... "I don't even care."... "Why should I?"... "I make my own choices and decisions."

Again he sits on the door entrance stairs, feeling a feeling of despair and a crushing weight of life. His Grandma shows up wearing her big and large white hat. She reaches down towards him.
"Come on."... "Early in the morning, you look very tired."... "What's going on with you?"
Lee steps back, inside the living room and glances at her, as she follows his footsteps, sitting on the sofa.
"Nothing Grandma, maybe the whole knight I did not sleep."
Twisting her neck, not to see him directly on his face, raises her right hand against her chest.
"By the way, father George was asking about you."
Raises his eyebrows at her, trying to be nicer, smiling at her sitting on the sofa, with his leg up on the coffee table. Crosses his hands above his belly.
"What did he say?"
Grandma feels more than a little disappointed, at least from her inside, easing herself into a big mirror.

"Nothing! He just wants to see you."

Having less to do with his feelings, about meeting the Pastor, he stands still on the ground.
"He'll see me, during my wedding time."
She struggles back into a sitting position, her eyes flickering, as she mentally reviews the situation. A different kind of shadow crosses her face.
"If you are not dead, you are still healthy."... "Wasting all your life for nothing!"... "Find your church friends if you can." She presses her lips together, clenches her hands and closes her eyes.
He shrugs, as if it didn't matter to him.
"I'm afraid for an ulterior motive, in asking you to return to church life."
He smiles rather sadly.
"I don't understand of what you are talking about, Grandma."

Though she wishes, to have more intimate connection, with her grandson, she deeply thinks about the idea of him, rambling on the street, striking her absurd.
"I mean, you are dead to church, but still alive and healthy to Garrison Blvd." she says, her voice trembling.
Lee rolls his eyes, looking away from her face.
"I don't want to be having this conversation with you."... "How many times do I have to tell you?"... "You are old enough to know about right and wrong."
Lee, he shrugs again, like it didn't matter to him.
"It's neither a healthy thing to repeat myself. "As our fathers say,"... "Don't implore to the Angels that don't listen". She repeats.
His eyes filled with regret, waves his hand on the air.
"I am sorry Grandma, I hear you of what you are saying."...
"I know what is making you angry."... "You don't seem very comfortable, with the way I am leading my life." He responds.
She straightens her big hat, moving it left and right.
"One who knows you better, buries you properly but I am not lucky. If you are rambling, the whole night like a hyena, how?"

Grandma, moves to the kitchen to prepare breakfast, as Lee steps towards the bathroom, to take a shower. His cell phone rings a dozen times, but his Grandma resists, not to pick up the calls. As he comes out from the bathroom, he follows one by one all miscalls, rolling and listening his messages.

She feels uneasy, thinking about who the caller may be.
"May I know who is calling you all this time?"
Tries to edge his way, around his business of selling drugs, his eyes fixed at his smartphone.
"Is personal Grandma." He says.
She attempts to sit down on a chair beside him, one more time confronting him in a comforting tone.
"I hope you are involved, in love affairs, aren't you?" She asks teasingly.
Rising to his feet from where he is sitting, tries to walk out.
"Not yet getting serious."

She stands straight and leans close to him, closing her eyes as there is nothing left to say.
"I don't see, all appears to be in order with you." She says. Lee tries to ease the situation, backing down not to stay on her way.
"I need some human company." He responds. In a doomed hope, lightly taps his shoulder, with her right fingers.
"You left the good company of the church, to join the dumb street of Garrison, for a reason of your own." He tries to step out several yards, towards the exit door. "It's a business." He says. She calms down, for the fear of the flood of emotions, might erupt.
"Of your own choice. An ill wind blowing in our neighborhood." She murmurs.

A strained silence follows and in this silence, Lee's mind is in Garrison Blvd. Grandma leading herself, to the rear of the dining room, looks down to the carpeted corridor, with a row of squares columns on the floor.
"Breakfast is ready." She pronounces in a low voice.
He looks at her sharply, trying to sit on the table. Lee enjoying the good smell of the food.
"Did you cook my favorite apple pie?"
Grandma, walks towards the fridge and slightly opens it, to see if there is any. In a short attention span, gazes at his face.
"No, the last piece, you have got it yesterday."

Lee's cell phone rings several times. As he sees the caller's name, he steps out few yards away, from his Grandma and by pressing talk, he starts to communicate with his friend Tim.
"Yo, where have you been?" Tim demands.
Lee as he chews the food, a particle of the food slides into his air track. His voice getting very serious, he coughs.
"Home, eating my breakfast yo." Lee responds.

I've been trying to call you a dozen times."... "What a fuck, you are doing there?"
Lee never giving much consideration to what he said, settles himself back in his seat, on a bench at the backyard. "Yo, don't make a fuss about nothing." Tim fishes out from his pocket, his little tiny plastic bag of weeds, as his wrapper falls down on the ground. Picks it from the ground, dusting it by rubbing against his thigh. "Yo, it is about business nothing less nothing more."

Lee, figures out, how upset his friend is, and finally, manages to cool down the argument. He stands still without getting furious, in a relaxed mood. "Sorry, I misheard you yo."

Moments later, Lee rushes driving his car towards Garrison Blvd. Wearing out his dark sunglasses on, looks right and left, on the cars front mirrors. After driving five minutes he parks near the BP gas station. Tim's stationed at the corner of the Gas Station, smoking his marijuana. Lee rushes out from his car and steps towards him.
"Excuse me, yo", Tim says, without greeting Lee.
Lee, raises his eyebrows at him.
"What were you doing all this time?" Tim asks.
Lee tries to be kind and nice in his response.
"Nothing, just relaxing."... "Doing my mutual job, yo."...
"To save and protect my ugly day yo."
That's what exactly, I thought you ware doing, yo. Tim responds, struggling back into a standing position.
Lee, inhales deep the smoke of the marijuana, in seconds to puff it out.

The Two Streets
NICKY'S HOME.

That night, Nicky, after staying long, rumbling on the street, with Lee, she drives home, feeling a mixed feeling, in regard to Lee's actions. Though she feels satisfied with Lee's care, she's not happy about his carelessness of the love affair. After ten minutes she reaches her house. She slowly walks upstairs, stepping towards her room. Her bed's messy, anyway she lurches over it, for a moment staring at the ceiling. Few minutes later she falls sleep, suddenly, to enter into the dream world. Her meeting with Lee at a bar, giving her a kiss, spells out in her dream.

Late in the morning, she wakes up from her small bed, wearing her night black dress. Sits on her bed, looking at the carpet between her feet moving it randomly, to search the sandals. Her adoptive mother Jenny, has taken off her sandals, for shower. Her voice trails off.
"God! I hate that."... "Who did it and why do they do it for me."... "Why mom wants to share my private things?"
Walk barefoot towards the bathroom cursing.
"Why the hell would she do it to me?" She yells.

After taking shower and dressing herself up, walks through the corridor very fast, just to meet her mother Jenny standing at the threshold of the door.
Meets Nicky at the door, as Nicky is glancing at her watch.
Both stare at each other.
"I am so glad to catch you before you left."... "Are you late for your school, Nicky?"
Nicky, miles back.
"Nods."
Jenny, crosses her hands over her belly.
"I would like to see you behaving like a student but-"
Nicky and her mother both sit on a couch side by side, as her mother try's to reach her hand.
"But see me what?"
Again Jenny, rests her arm over her shoulder.
"I'm trying, to be gentle with you."... "If you can come up, with some reasons, of why you are always late. You know, right now I am angry and upset."...."You will not get cured, if you hide your wounds."... "Am I right or wrong?"

In a hurry, Nicky tries to step down the stairs, as Jenny is locking, the front door of the house.
"Am I hiding! Hiding what?"... "I have nothing to rebel against you, Mom."... "Right now, I don't want to be

judgmental."... "I wonder, if you ever get to my point." Jenny, takes a deep breath of let it go, looking at her coldly. "You're the master at keeping secrets."... "But it's not a healthy thing."... "I'm forced to police you myself."

The Two Streets
THE STREET I BELONG.

When his mother's womb relaxed for seven years, after which her pregnancy surprised all the neighborhood, Mike's conceived. He's born seven years after the last son. He becomes the last son of seven. He checks his mother's womb, before her womb said enough, and became a clear fact to be born, on this planet. His parents never expected the pregnancy to happen. When it happened, they spontaneously accepted it with a happy attitude. His mother said "Yes", to bear him in her womb and his father, became pregnant in his mind. After nine month, he becomes natural. The year was 1957.

He was lucky enough, to be baptized, in the Parish of St. Michael. His birth, renewed his mother's life. It gave her a new life and a particular discipline. He was keenly aware, that he was being accepted with different care and renewed spirit.

The town of his birth place is called, "Keren", located in the middle of Eritrea's Low land. Keren is surrounded by four big mountains. North, Mt. Lalumba, South, Mt. Ziban, East, Mt. Etabir and West, Mt. Senkil. A military base known by the Italian name "Forto" (Fortress), is In the middle of the town. It's built by the Turkish some time five hundred years ago. The main street, where Mike grew up, is called "Keren Lalai". It extends from "Forto", to the church of St. Micael.
Mike, liked a lot of things about his neighborhood, Keren Lalai. He doesn't want to put it out of his heart. After all, it was this neighborhood that fashioned his mind.

* * * * * * * * *

Mike, braided like Rasta, trolls his luggage with his backpack on his shoulder, walking down the corridor at BWI Airport. After a long walk he slides towards the public bathroom. He tries by mistake to step towards female bathroom. Suddenly, he meets with a young white Lady at the threshold. "Oh, oh wrong place. It's female ones." She yells. "I'm sorry." Mike says, softly. He backs stepping back word. Very thoughtful, his eyes fixed looking at the ceiling, he starts to talk to himself, like in a day dream, shaking his head right and left.
"Babur e gebeyki" (The train it's not your way). He says, expressing himself in a local saying. "Wrong place." He repeats, Stepping towards the male bathroom.

As he gets out of the public bathroom, he tries to lie down on one of the benches stretching his legs over his bag. "Am I on the right place for this kind of life? Could I exist, in the land of all things functions?" Sits in a sitting position. "Too early to complain! As our fathers say "Whether to bake or not, one must reach the water". Let me see and wait, of what America will offer to me."

The Two Streets
GARRISON MY FATE STREET.

A busy urban street, traffic is loud, city sounds fill the air. Mike, steps of a local bus, luggage in tow. He gets down from the bus and walks several steps down the sidewalk in Garrison Blvd., a street filled with awful of marijuana scent.

The street is packed, with men and women with their children. A grid of mini colored lights shines, on the sidewalk, as a high volume music bombards the street. Mike is awed by his surroundings and becomes lost for a moment, until a Rude Man, snaps him back into reality, by shoving Mike and calling him a racial slur. Rude man imagining himself, as one of the elite people and not liking the color of his skin, approaches him in a total rage tone.
"Yo! Nigger!" He yells.
Mike, struggles back into a standing position, staring at the Rude Man reviewing the situation.
"Original Nigger!" He responds, in an angry tone.
Mike, tries to keep himself silent, raising his eyebrows and saying nothing.
The Rude Man, shakes his head, in a mock sadness and attempts to step towards him.
"Original! Original! Who's the photocopy!" He yells again.
Mike, bows his head down, looking at him side way.
"I never signed any contract that I know with you."... "No need to get mad at me.".... "I don't know you and you don't know me."... "Why you're so upset with me? I didn't say any bad things to you."
The Rude Man, looks at him coldly, feeling like desperate. "Whatever"! If I don't like the color of your eyes!" Again he glares at his face. "I mean what I mean. Face it damn nigger!"
His voice trailing off, Mike, puts his fist against his lips. "You take what it belongs to you. I am only trained to bless rather than to curse!"
"Go back to where you came from!"
Mike, turning his face down for seconds, he shakes his head, taking a deep breath. "Believe me! The stone you throw to the sky, breaks your head."

Attempts to disregard the Rude man, by straightening his shoulders up, walks away from the Rude man, literally speechless. When he reaches at BP gas station he crosses the parking lot. He picks his way, over to the store stepping slowly, as he is intercepted, by young African American female, who

wanted his attention. He brushes and passes her, without saying a single word, bowing his head towards the sidewalk pavement. Still immersed into a deep thought, standing straight, he eyes the young female girl, looking up and down. "Early in the morning, to see the bad and the good." He says, trying not to think about the Rude man's actions.
"He absolutely is a bastard. This is the meanest thing anyone's ever done to me."

DON'T PUSH ME.

On a hot August morning, Nicky wakes up from her bed and slips on to search her bed shoes. With her nightgown over she heads stepping down the stairs, in a tip-toe, not to make a noise, to wake up her adoptive parents. She takes a deep breath and pulls open the wooden door, half way. Walks out, with her cell phone on her hand, ready to call Lee.
"Where're you?" She asks in a yelling tone.
"The same place" Lee responds calmly.
"Your world!" She chuckles.
"I'm just connected to the street for my own reasons," he says, admitting her chuckle.
"The cursed street!" she giggles.
"No the blessed one", he counters.
"For me it's a weird street". She says, hanging up the phone.
She gets annoyed all over again, for Lee not being honest.

Four hours later, after getting ready, doing her hair and putting all the beauty stuff, without telling Lee, she surprises him, driving her car to meet him at the Gas station. Lee's outside, standing near one of pumps. She stands, cross-armed in front of him. He looks at her, his face twitched. She forced a smile, looking at him sideway.
She steps closer to him.
"I want to have more fun, other than rambling on the street", she says, in whisper tone, leaning against his ear.
"Where?" he responds.
"To the swimming pool" she says.
He pauses for seconds, as his mind starts to protest.
"Okay" he says.
"Well, I know you're upset... ".
He snaps. "I'm not upset".
Both drive to the swimming pool.

At the place, Lee and Nicky sit on a bed like chair, both viewing towards the water pool. There, one can see, deep inside the clean water, the trees and the surrounding light poles, filtered through the water.
Lee, looks down the water, as Nicky is looking up towards the blue sky, still laying comfortably, on the stretched flat bed chair.
"I came here, just to accompany you."... "I myself have never been in the water, let alone to swim."... "I spent all my time rambling on the street of Garrison."

"By the way do you swim?"
Suddenly, she walks towards the water, stepping on the shallow water.
"Indeed I know! My father taught me how, when I was little."

Nicky, invites him to join her to the water, smiling at Lee.
"Come on! Where I am is not deep!"... "It's shallow. Let's enjoy it together."...
"This time forget Garrison, let us enjoy each other."
"Sink or swim"! He chuckles. She turns around frantically, paddling towards Lee, floating on the water.
"Do you have a Hydro-phobia? My mind can't digest it! If you are not scared from Garrison bullets, how in the world you get afraid of the water."

Lee, smoking his cigar, squeezing weakly closes his eyes.
"Are you okay!"... "You got somewhere lost."... "You better get found."... "You need help and I am not the one to give you either."
Sounding shrill and helpless, even a little scared, she slumps against one of the electric pole.
"What f...ck. I hurt myself!
"Don't blame me." Lee says.
"Just go please! We can talk about it, some other times. For now leave me alone."

The Two Streets
AMIDST A WAR ZONE.

It is obvious, that this is Mike's first time, in a large city. He makes his way down the crowded sidewalk, taken in his surroundings, looking much like a tourist. Mike finds himself in front of a rundown motel. Because of a long walk under a sun, breathing harshly and his forehead covered in sweat, he approaches the Clerk Woman, as she is doing her normal work. Walks in and in a thick East African accent, interacts with the Clerk woman.
"Hi! Do you have an available room mom? What will be the weekly rate?" Mike asks her, smiling genuinely.

Reaching out into her purse and pulling out a pen, she extends her greetings.
"Yes we have." she says, a smile radiating on her face. Again, she gazes at his face. "By the way, you don't look from this area?" Mike, rocking back and forth on his feet, gives her a sweet smile.
"How do you know?"
The Clerk, trying to figure out, what answer to give to him, delivers the room key to him, with a smile.
"By your accent!"

Mike is taken to a dingy room, equipped with a small television set and an automatic coffee maker. Mike Settles in for the night. Listens to the sounds, outside his window, all the yelling, gunshots, car horns honking and people shouting. "This place really is a war zone!"... "I didn't know, I was going to be in a bad place."... "I feel terrible being here." He picks out from his pocket, a photo of the street he grew up, again and again gazing at the picture.
"Ah! The paradise I dreamed about when it turns to be hell!"
"From that one this one is the worst." he says, comparing life in Baltimore to his own town.
He takes a photograph of his family, from his luggage. Sits on the bed and brings the photo, close to his heart. Kisses the photo one by one.
"I wish I made a second thought, for not immigrating, to the USA."

Rummages through his bag and retrieves a calling card. He looks out, through a small window of his motel room and spots a payphone down below. Looks right and left out of fear, holding the phone on his hand.
"Hi mom! I know, that you all miss me!"
"We all miss you. How is USA?"

Hiabu Hassebu

Arranges his braided hair, gazing at the payphone machine. "For now all seems functioning, but still I'm distracted by the nostalgia, of my own people and hometown."

The Two Streets
THANKSGIVING EVE.

It's the eve of Thanksgiving day. Lee's as usual on the street of Garrison, together with his gangs group, smoking and chatting, loudly. Nicky, finding herself so preoccupied wit Lee she drives towards Garrison. There she sees Lee from a distant. She calls his name in a yelling tone.
Lee, steps towards her.
"I hope you're aware what date is tomorrow?" She asks in a whisper tone.
In a half-joking manner, "It's a normal day, 365 days minus 1" he says.
"You mean you can't sense it differently", she asks.
"I sense all days the same, nothing a special for me", he responds.
Nicky's is more concerned about her love relationship.
She sighs.
"I don't see why," she voices.
"At least can you sacrifice a few hours with me?" She adds. "I'm sorry for that",… "One can't climb two trees because one has two legs" he adds, feeling sarcastically.
"I need your attention" she says, exploding in anger.
He crosses his arm over his chest.
"Well, I feel actually, we're not on the same page", she says, in a low voice.
"The same page" he repeats, sadly, fumbling for another cigarette.
Suddenly, she feels innocent.
"Can you do me a favor?" She asks.
"What favor?" He responds.
"Just to go go to a Disco bar", suggests, laying her right hand across her forehead.
Lee agrees to her proposal and drive towards the Disco-house.
Lee and Nicky are inside a Disco house, sitting on tall chairs, in front of a bar. One could smell all the stink of the bar. Lee, with an open bottle of beer in his hand, is watching a football game on TV, listening to the loud music of Hip-hop bombarding the place. At the corner of the Discohouse, some people are dancing. Suddenly, Nicky invites Lee to dance with her. Her voice gets deep and resonant, lifting herself up to the stage.
"Come on Lee! Let us enjoy dancing. I want to get to my feet, to exult in this and feel happy."
His voice has gone strange and croaky.
"I myself want to be myself right now."… "I'm busy with watching the football match. As for you, I will let you free

to dance."
"Get away from you own world, I mean Garrison. You are only trying to edge your way, out around me.

Both, walk out from the disco-house, through the exit door, looking puzzled, even worried as they file out the door.

The Two Streets
THE DAY I MET THE DRUG LORD.

Lee wearing his black tattered jeans, with blue shirt and white collars, is sitting on his own in a restaurant, at Liberty Height.
At the threshold of the restaurant, Mike is silently and politely standing, to get his sit by one of the Waitress.
The Waitress, opening wide, the white decorated plastic curtain, she steps towards Mike, just in time, leading Mike his way towards an empty table.
"Welcome! For how many seats? Gentle man.
From inside of the restaurant, standing halfway from where he is sitting, Lee claps his hands. Pulls his jacket out, draping it on the back of his chair, pointing with his finger to an empty chair.
"Here, here there is an empty place. He can sit with me."
A deep look of concern crosses on her face.
"Do you know the person who is waving his hand?" she asks.

His mind so wrapped up, to capture the stranger's invitation, in a straight glance, steps towards Lee.
"Not really, but who knows he might know me. Early acquaintance might be for good or bad."
The Waitress leads Mike cordially, towards Lee's table.
Lee, in a surprise and warm welcoming mood, shakes his hand.
"Welcome to our Garrison neighborhood."
He squeezes his hand and doesn't let it go.
"I like your accent."
Mike, keeps gazing at Lee.
Lee tries to light a fresh cigarette.
He looks over at him and pulls a chair with a respect.
"Take a seat" and enjoy my company."

The Waitress, lays down the forks and the dishes on the table, glancing at both of them at the same time.
"How well do you know each other?"
Lee gazes at her.
"Well, I don't need to know anyone, just to associate myself with one."... "I's a coincidence, I liked his Angel, I just read innocence on him."
Lee, casts a quick glance around, to assure him his friendship as he grabs his wrist.
"My genuine pleasure to meet you!"... "I'm sure that me and my people are going to protect you Mike."
Mike, waves his right and left arm to the air.
"God forbid!"... "What kind of protection you are speaking about?"... "You are just scaring me."... "I don't have an

enemy that I know, to be protected from."
His curiosity flipping into the red zone, Lee, looks at his face blankly.
"Garrison is a place where you don't know your enemy or your friend."... "We reason with a gun, that have no politics."... "Do you want to join my club?"

Mike, gazes at him curiously, in an air of disbelief.
"Let me process my awareness of the neighborhood first, before I join your club."... "For now as an immigrant, It's enough for me to work and manage to survive."... "I have a family to take care of."
Lee, re-affirming his offer, he pauses for seconds, moving his eyes up and down, quickly. His voice taking into a faint teasing edge, he slightly smiles.
"You know Mike, I don't like the street neither, I joined it only for a reason."
Mike, feels sorry, in an instinct asking mood.
"For what reason?" He asks.
Lee, swallows hard.
"For a simple reason of a revenge."... "I'm a product of this neighborhood and both of my parents were killed by unknown assassins."

Both look at one another, as Mike responds with a nod.
"I see what is happening, on the street of Garrison and understand of what you went through in your life."
When both finish eating, they step out of the restaurant, Lee remains behind and heads to the counter, to pay the Bill. They walk out from the restaurant, through the front door stepping down the stairs. onto the sidewalk of Garrison Blvd. Both stop, just before they reach, the corner of the BP store. Lee looks left and right, as Mike follows his footsteps.
Mike, glances at the big rosary, hanging on Lee's neck.
"You're Catholic, I guess."
Lee, decides to let it go, without trying to give him, a further explanation, of his real faith issue.
"Born but not a practicing one."
Mike, takes out his small rosary from his pocket.
"Me too I am Catholic." He says.
Lee, tries to get a reading of their conversations, showing in his face, a face of interest.
"The reason I am here with you today, is to recruit you, I mean if the word recruit is normal."

The Two Streets

Mike his eyes popped open, pauses for seconds.
"Recruit you what! How?"
Lee, tries to turn the question, around the way he wanted.
"To be part of the neighborhood, I mean Garrison neighborhood."
Mike, gives him a long stare.
"I am just setting my foot, to this neighborhood and I don't like the way this conversation is heading." ... "I suspect, I know what your plans are."... "I'm a lonely immigrant, living like a crazy in my dream land."

Despite everything Mike said, he tries to make him stop thinking bad.
"I know you have no friends, no family in here, but don't let yourself, to be the orphan of the town. The future will be ruled, only by your present attitude."
Finally, Mike pulls over the street of Garrison. He slowly walks towards the store, his mind re-running the long conversation he had with King Lee. Sounding almost sad, talks to himself in a low voice.
"I wish he told me, in a more detail about it, whether to be recruited or not."... "Really, I'm confused."
Mike, just checking the area, he looks right and left.
"I give my resignation, before I am hired."... "No one joins a war with his eyes open, without knowing the risks."
Lee, steps on the opposite side of the street. Arguing with himself, not knowing precisely of what he meant by his say.
"I don't know, what made him say this way."... "Might be, it is the loneliness and sorrow, that motivated him to express so."

Lee, pulls himself, from the street and steps towards the BP Gas station store. From the opposite side of the street, he sees Tim walking slowly down the street, towards him. As they meet, Lee speaks to his friend Tim, about the newcomer, Mike, the immigrant, to Garrison neighborhood. Tim, curls his upper lip.
"By the way, are you planning to hire him now?"... "I hate to disappoint you boss."... "Does he understand the business, the Garrison way. Our way. King Lee's way."
Tim's cell phone buzzes, as he flips it open, still his attention being with Lee, then putting it back away.
"How come he be part of us or how can he be on board, if he doesn't smoke marijuana."... "By the way, does he speak English? I hope he does."
Lee, pulls a Black and Mild cigar, from his pocket and puts it into his mouth, without lighting it. Not to interrupt his suggestions,

he takes a long look at Tim.
"Don't worry, I will get him involved, in a different way. I know how to recruit."

* * * * * * * * *

The Two Streets
NO FUN WITH A GUN.

Blood pounding in his veins, holding himself in check, to consider Lee's words, Mike stands in front of the BP Gas station door, as he tries to open the door. He enters the store and steps towards the switch light behind the door, to turn on the light of the shabby store. He stands straight, stretching his arms high above his head, strolling over the window, looking out onto the street. "I hope I'm not dealing
with the wrong people."
Having assured himself, that there are no customers, the street being clear, he steps away from the window and sits on a chair.
"I hope I espouse a peaceful integration to the American society. That is my stance I assume. No fun with a
gun and life with the gangs."
He shrugs, as his Rasta braided long hair, falls in the middle of his chest.
"I miss my hometown Keren. I am afraid if I am able to
handle, my situation of being an immigrant."
Looks up the daily files. Suddenly, his family photo falls down on the ground. From where he is sitting, he bows down and collects the photo, getting ready to kiss it.
"There's no good thing about being alone and lonely. I miss
you all."
Putting the photo in front of him, drinks water from the bottle, laid on his side tray table.
Closes the files and in his mind immersed into a deep thought, he gets connected to his past life.
"I was alright and fine, while I was living at home."... "I wish I knew all the risks beforehand, before I came to live in Baltimore, as an immigrant."
A pang of sorrow shoots through his mind.
"It's my choice, no one to be blamed, though I came into this life of undeclared war, not with my eyes open."

Back in time, his memories of the past two decades, floods into his mind. The long hours, he spends, inside the store, day and night, without a day off, made him complain about his life. He invites his mind to rewind, to the old times, living in his home town. It's the middle of August of 2012. Mike's heading to Las Vegas, to pitch his first book, "Fagret: the female survivor", to a Hollywood producer. The eve before his departure day, while he's busy, in the store, Nicky shows up for her own needs. Nicky, never come to the store, unaccompanied by Lee. She greets Mike, with a big smile.

"Where's Lee, your body?", Mike, asks. Nicky, points her finger, towards Lee's car.
"He's there in the car", she responds. "Hurry, Lee's waiting me".... "Give me a Dutch Master", she says, staring down her lower body. After, he gives her needs, "You look, "chic ala mode" (Beautiful, to the style), he express, in French. Not, understanding, of what mike said, she quickly, gives her back to Mike, stepping slowly towards the car. Mike, still contemplating her beauty, "What a beauty?"...
"God given structure" he says, to himself. He sits down on a chair. "Oh, the first copy, of her creator", he repeats.

After his stay in Las Vegas, for four days, he flies back to Baltimore. The next morning, while Mike's busy working in the store, by chance Nicky shows up at the store. It's the first time to see Mike, all dressed with ties over.
Getting surprised, "Mike you look good", she expresses, smiling widely.
Mike's still navigating in his mind, the unique beauty of Las Vegas. He return a smile at her, and greets her.
"Job interview", she exclaims.
"Coming from Las Vegas", he responds.
"Lucky, you're Mike!" she says. "In my life, I've never been, out Baltimore", she adds, feeling somewhat not happy. Mike, stares at her face, again with a big smile. "Believe me heaven's there", he says, though knowing, exaggerating.

The Two Streets
BP MY WORK DESTINATION.

Two weeks later, after Lee met with Mike, he plans to make, a car wash event on the compound of the Gas station. He's sitting in his car, for dusk to fall. He gives in an already wrapped marijuana and lights it. When night's to catch up he drives towards the gas station. Wearing his jogging suit, with his sunglasses in his hand, steps fast towards the store's main door. Without knocking the door he surprises
Mike, who is doing his daily job as a clerk.
"Am I late Mike?"
Mike tries to smile.
Lee, hands the copy of the agreement, putting it on top of his desk.
"I know you are new to this business, Mike. Are you excited?"
Mike, looking down, he starts to read, through the copy of papers, with not much interest.
"I don't get easily excited by my nature but first I would like to see the results."... "Written things until they are materialized, never ever give, an effect to my soul."
At a spotlight, Mike looking over at Lee, stares at his face.
"Promise, no drug selling at the event."... "I don't want any trouble."
Lee, sits on the armchair across from Mike, answering to his point, reflexively.
"I respect the excuses of all your fears, and I agree with you Mike."... "I know, you always want to do the right thing."
Mike, lights an air freshener, sitting back to his chair.
"I will do whatever I can, as far as the rules and regulations of my station are respected."
Lee, though he feels very challenged, still he feels excited.
"Count on me Mike, after all it is a business, a Win Deal."
Lee, shakes his hand and walks out with excitement.
"Remember the date is next Saturday. See you then, you will get surprised."

* * * * * * * * * *

Lee, walks down the street of Garrison, suddenly to hear a voice calling his name. Lee, turns his head around, to see, who his caller is. He slowly walks, crossing Garrison street, to meet Rob, in front of the Hair Saloon shop. Both start to share, about the dirty business, suddenly, to see, two young ladies, sneaking out through the door, both arguing in a loud tone.

"Leave me alone", Gene screams, wearing in a mini-skirt.
"Bull shit", Ashely responds, yelling.
"Give me my money, that you owe me", Gene, again screams.
"Come on girl".... "I know, what I owe you",... "Just give me time to pay you back", Ashely responds. King Lee and Rob approach them, stepping few yards.
"Beautiful girls, don't fight on the street," Rob voices.
"Stay out of our affairs!" Ashely, responds.
King Lee, pauses and looks around, as he pretends to be latching his shoes, bowing down. "All war starts with pussy and money", Lee says, chuckling.
"Powerful and impressive idea", Gene replies. "But in Garrison, the drug mixes it", She adds.
"How? Lee asks. "In Garrison, the money always circulates, while the pussy stuff's in constant fear", Gene, explains. "You guys, somehow, restored our peace", Ashley says, smiling at both.
"I need your phone number", Lee asks politely.
Both "nod", giving their numbers, to Lee.
"Right now, I would like to hire you- Lee, says.
"Hire where?" Ashely, interrupts him.
"Next week, I've a car wash event, right here at BP Gas station",... "You're selected to help me, as Bikini to wash cars", Lee says.
Both agree, "Okay".
"And thank you, for making our day", Ashely, expresses.

The Two Streets
YOU DON'T CLAIM THE PLACE.

Two Lee's gangs with Tim, are staying together inside a bar. At the corner of the bar under the stage, three males and a female are entertaining the customers of the day. Most of the customers are from the same neighborhood, all wearing a white T-shirt with their varied colors of jeans. Suddenly a Stranger man, wearing a black T-shirt, shows up at the bar sitting alone on a table. All eyes fall on the stranger man. Without saying and commenting anything he approaches the stranger man from behind.
"Yo nigger! You are in the wrong place." Tim yells.
The Stranger, gazes at him with a penetrating gaze.
"Wrong place! There is no right place in Garrison!
Tim, steps forward and stands straight before him, within a distance of nose to nose.
"I am just giving you a choice, to leave the place immediately, if not-"
The Stranger, steps back few yards away.
"You don't claim this place either."

Lee is outside standing in the dark, near the dumpster under a tree, smoking his last piece of marijuana, while Tim is in a heated dialogue with the Stranger man. After he finishes his smoke, he walks in to the bar slowly, he approaches the stranger from behind.
He stands close to his eyes.
"Hey man, what are you doing here?"
The Stranger, raises his hood high enough, to expose his face, with his fist ready to fight and defend himself.
"I was born and grew up here and I don't have an enemy that I know, to tell me what I have to do or not."

Lee, trembles with anger and shouts at his face.
"Don't you know you are in a wrong place. This is my territory, King Lee's territory."
Pulls his gun out and points to his face.
"The two of us can't exist, on the same street. If you want to stay alive, it is your choice."... "This place is only allowed for the WHITE SHIRT group, unless you want to join my company."... "Right now if you demonstrate your fidelity to us, you can save your life."

Lee, pulls his gun away from his face, still holding it on his right hand.
"If you ever come again to my territory, you will face the

fact. I mean my bullets."
The Stranger, tries not to show his fears.
"Do you really expect me to join your company?"... "Not all who wear the black shirt are your rival gangs, as you believe."... "You are fighting with an innocent resident, of the neighborhood. Am I wrong?"
Both walk out from the bar, stepping down towards the dumpster. As they are discussing, near the dumpster, in a total darkness, Tim follows them.
"I don't care! The last good word, you hear from me. It is the last and the end of my say."

Lee, again reaches his gun.
"Now let us talk about it while we are off camera. Do you know, what you will get in return? A bullet that have no politics in your head."
The Stranger, who is also on his feet, lowers his eyes, to avert Lee's angry gaze.
"One, who wants to act, never tells his mother and I am not afraid to die. If that is of what you are worried about."

Tim, jumps onto him, when a sharp look from Lee, falls on to the Stranger, as he puts himself in between Lee and him.
"You are one of the rival infiltrator gang members, you happen to be here just to infiltrate our base." He gets angry at him, for he crossing the line.
"All you need to know is, that you are talking, with a son of a bitch number one killer, King Lee."

Lee, holds his voice for a moment and looks with a stern warning, looking at him.
"Yo, watch your back. Resisting my order won't do you any good. You won't get out alive."

The Stranger, raises his both hand, pulling up his shirt sleeves, with fist on the air.
"Neither my hand is holding water. You may kill me but you will lose your business, trying to murder an innocent man."
Lee, yells at his face and points his gun at his forehead.
"Yo, respect me. I am a professional killer. I won't allow you to walk into my territory. If I want I can kill you outright." The Stranger, nods rapidly, to make Lee understand, how much he means it.
"Are you under the influence of drugs. Why you attack innocent people. Are you created to kill and destroy only." Red rage

gripping King Lee, he grabs him with his neck and shakes him until his teeth rattle in his head.
"I'll break your neck."

Lee bows down, to see, his big rosary falls down on the ground. He immediately, puts his gun back to its place and collects his rosary.
"As I am engaged with drugs in an invisible war, I need to reason why?" Something stops him, that he is not aware of, as he cools down from acting. "This's not of my own will, there is something behind it."
Before putting back his rosary to his neck, he kisses it. Suddenly he is immersed into a deep thought, as the pictures of his childhood, with his Grandma comes to his mind, reciting all silently.

Hiabu Hassebu
THE DEAL.

On the event of car wash day, early in the morning Lee drives towards the Gas station. He parks his car at the corner of the store, dozens young girls with BIKINI (18-20) are standing, before the entrance of the store, all anxious to meet Lee, among themselves talking loud and excited. Wearing his white T-shirt and the sun glass on his left hand, he makes his steps, to the gas station.

All the BIKINI girls are gathered together, as he steps towards th em.
"Are you ready, the beautiful and gentle ladies of Garrison."
Not to lose the good mood of Lee, all smile feeling the most potent feeling of joy.
"Yes, indeed King Lee!" they respond in one voice.
Lee, puts his sunglasses on and turns his head 360 degrees, gazing in a smile at all of them.
"No need of any kind of a rehearsal, only half an hour of my directions, is enough, I think."

All smile at the same time, walking and stepping backward. He gives his brief direction and his offer for the job, with all the BIKINI girls surrounding him, wearing their colorful mini-skirts.

Raises his pen to the air and lifts the agreement paper on his hand.
"All tips with your job allowance are yours, the rest is mine. Do you agree on that?"

One of the Bikini girls, steps forward and muses banging her legs out of joy, to answer him, in a sudden joyful response.
"We all agree, ready for the job."

Another Bikini girl, getting serious about what matters in their deal, asks Lee in a scared tone.
"No other side job please. I mean, Selling your stuff, the drugs. I hate to be in jail."
Lee's face looks defiant, to keep things straight and clear, he takes his eyes over to her. He steps few yards away from the Bikini girl's and turns back to answer her, in a confident loud tone.
"Leave everything to me and I promise, I will not let you down, just do what you are assigned to do. See you then."

The same day, of a car wash day, Nicky, gets ready to go for shopping, to MONDAWMIN MALL. After she eats her breakfast

and feeds her cat, wearing a sleek black suit and a high heel shoes, walks to sit on the sofa. Takes out all her beauty stuff, from her purse and lays them all on a small table, adjacent to the sofa, with a small mirror on her hand smiling with herself. Cleans her face with a soft paper, again looking at her face through the mirror.
"What an amazing day? Right time to do my shopping."
With the car key on her hand, she looks through the window, to check the whether of the day. The day is bright and warm. As she feels the breeze coming off the water, laden with moisture, it refreshed her mind. Opens her car and starts the engine, as she drives in reverse.
"Let the day be my day."

She reaches the MALL, quietly enters through the main door. Heads towards the clothing department, in a tip-toe, and starts to browse, the cloth of her own wear and style. Picks her stuff and walks towards the counter, to pay her bills.

After she pays her bills, steps fast down the corridor. As she reaches the exit gate, one of the Rival Gangs, from the BLACK SHIRT 66, approaches behind her.
"You ugly little girl, you better stop hanging with the selfproclaimed king Lee."... "We're after him and no one will save him from our bullets."... "Garrison will be either for us or for him." he yells.
Nicky, looks back at him, staring with a stern face.
"Move away from me! I don't give dumb shit to anyone who tries to scare me." The Rival gang, in a choking sound, steps forward-looking at her, face to face.
"Save your life! There is no time, to play the game of hide-and-seek."
Nicky, touches her belt with her hand, gazing at him sternly.
"King Lee's belt is always fastened, to fight with you cowards the unfastened belt. Try it but you will get it."

As their arguments cools down, Nicky walks calmly towards her car. The Rival gang member, leaves her alone on the parking lot, walking on the other direction of the MALL.

Nicky, after a short drive on Liberty Height street, she reaches Garrison Blvd. She pulls her car to the BP gas station, where the event of car wash, is taking place. Lee is busy and all his attention is with the BIKINI girls. Suddenly, Nicky sees Lee, with one of the BIKINI girl, hugging and kissing. She stands

straight on her feet and looks King Lee from distant. Her demeanor changes instantly, her feet and legs shaking. Walks up few yards forward towards
Lee, her mind getting troubled.
"It's such a disgusting day, to see all this crappy things."
Lee gets surprised by the presence of Nicky, which he didn't anticipate. He looks down to the ground, trembling in fear of her retribution. After few seconds, raises his head up to control her, looking at her straight on her face.
"Why is it, that your fucking evil spirit following me, wherever I go? You better behave."

Nicky, hunches forward in an angry tone of voice.
"I feel very uncomfortable of all your weird actions. I need to reach the root of your hidden mysteries.
Are you turning your back to me, to break our relation."
Again she frowns at his face.
"What kind of a boyfriend you are?"... "I am glad that I caught you with my eye." Lee, looks straight at her face and answers her delicately, believing in his mind, that she is out of her mind.
"Sometimes I am afraid, you're looking for answers to the questions that have none."

* * * * * * * * *

I'M OKAY, YOU'RE OKAY.

It's late in the morning and Nicky's standing on a bus stop, waiting for Lee to pick her up. Her mother Jenny, shows up walking down the Liberty road from east. Jenny, as she reaches where, Nicky's standing, she greets her.
"Good morning".
Nicky, responds "Good morning".
Jenny, wrapping her arm on Nicky's shoulder, "Are you still well and safe, rumbling on the street", she says.
Nicky, appreciating the comfort of her Mom's gentle touch, "I'm Okay", she responds.
Jenny, stepping back and glancing at her face, "where're you going?" she asks.
"To the Mall", Nicky responds, looking at her wrist watch, trying to see the time.
Jenny, pauses for seconds, gazing at her face, affectionately. "Same destination! I'll follow you", she says.
Nicky snaps. "Follow me! What?" she responds, in a loud tone.
Jenny, shook her head, while trying to pull her into her arms.
"I'm not baby, I'm 18 now", Nicky, reacts in fear.
"It's nothing about me", responds, in a deep thought, in her mind, complaining, about the bad life on Garrison street.
"I hope, you didn't start to drink, the infected water of Garrison", she adds, thinking with whom she associate with.
Nicky, responds angrily, "What do you mean by that?" she asks.
"I mean the holy water of Garrison", she repeats, chuckling.
"I like my company" Nicky says, in a whisper.
"The company of Garrison wonderers", she sighs. Nicky after chatting for a while, she yawns, because of the repetitions. "I'm not enjoying our chat" she says, walking away from her.

* * * * * * * * * *

A police car pulls into the parking area, where Lee's parking. Lee honks, several times. Nicky, runs towards Lee's car. Lee unlocks the car's door, as he see, Nicky, rushing towards him. Right away, she opens the door and sits next to Lee, without saying anything. Lee his eyes widely open, one time he focusses to see, the parked police car, behind his car. Pretending to be like a good guy, he picks a newspaper and attempts to read. The police car pulls back in reverse and leave the area. Lee, breathes out deeply, feeling relived. He puts his sun glass over his forehead. He, looks at Nicky side way, as he lowers the volume of the speaker. He smiles at her.

"With whom were you chatting?" He asks, in a low voice, whispering. Interrupting him and glancing straight at his face, "with my Mom", she responds.
"You mean your real Mom", He interjects, reciting in his mind, the reality of the fact, knowing Jenny being her adoptive mother.
"Yes my real mother", she responds, in a low voice.
"May I know the name of your Mom? He asks, wearing again his sun glass. She gets angry. "None of your business", she yells.

* * * * * * * * * *

The Two Streets

IT'S YOUR FAULT, IF I'M ON THE STREET.

It's Mr. Derik, the real reason, for Nicky's life, to make her fall into and be trapped, to the Garrison way of life. Nicky, as she's bright and very beautiful lady, she's not able to continue with her higher studies, due to the drinking problem of her adoptive father. It's unnatural, to have a father, whose, his drinking habit, day in and out, is increasing. He becomes, a constant source of embarrassment, to the whole family. Jenny, his wife sees, the change of his behavior, going to the opposite direction. He being rude and awful, the least she can do's, to push herself, towards arguments. As an adoptive parents, they don't have a child of their own. That's why they adopted Nicky, when Nicky was one year old.

The dark cloud of un-certainty, hanging over the neighborhood of Garrison's another reason, that hindered families, to take care of their children. Many families, they have optioned, either to live struggling, or flee from the area. Nicky's parent, would have liked to flee the area rather than to stay, if it was for Nicky's involvement, in love affair with the drug dealer, Lee. One morning, she gets up early from her bed. As life became the most lasting much to her irritation, She approaches him, forcing herself to the present situations. She sighs, gazing at his face, "All seems, you have forgotten your job".
Surprised by her words, "which job?" He responds.
Again, she sighs, keeping her head straight and staring at him. "The promise we made at our wedding". She says. "I'm kind lost, tell me which one which", he says.
"It's only one", she giggles.
"So tell me instead of telling me in a puzzle", he responds, raising his voice.
"Either integrate, to Garrison way or flee the area", she says. "I love the the place, I occupy, I'm Garrisonian", he brags. She, sighs and gazes at his face again. "You don't
like to risk, moving, do you?"
"No I don't".
Nicky, nagging on the wrong neighborhood of Garrison, wakes up from her sleep, as both parents are arguing in a loud tone. She steps down the stairs, wearing her night garments.
Approaches them standing over Mr. Derik, looking side way, Jenny.
Mr, Derik, screws up his face.
Jenny, looks distressed.

"Oh, I'm sorry to wake you up". She says, coughing, then quiet.
"I heard all kinds of noises on the street".... "That would
be enough for me". Nicky, says, sounding mournful.
Nicky, wipes her face and tilted down her head towards her Dad.
He leans down, looking at Nicky.
"What's going on with you guys? Nicky, says in a low voice.
"We're just arguing, about not loosing our future", Jenny,
responds.
"Loosing our future!", Nicky, echoes.
"I mean, your Daddy, don't like to risk, moving", Jenny,
explains.
"Do you mean to change to other location?, She asks.
"Yes, indeed!", Jenn repeats, shaking her head gloomily.
"There's no safe place in this dumb city", he intervenes. Seeing,
the mess of Garrison street, "I'm kind scared", Jenny, responds.

The Two Streets
THE TRICKY ACT.

It's a bright Sunday. Jenny, wakes up from her sleep, getting ready to go for the service. After taking a shower, well vested she consumes her breakfast. She drives her car, as she's accompanied, by a soft spiritual classical music. On her way, she pulls to the BP gas station, for a refill of gasoline. Suddenly, a teenager with a loud noise of Hip-hop parks, parallel to her car. The music's pounding the area like a bomb. "Oh, my Lord" she says, putting her fingers, to both of her ears, if she can ever tap, the horrible sound.
She steps forward, towards the Mini-store to pay for her gas. She greets Mike.
"Good morning".
On the left side of the store, she sees a Handicap man, sitting on his wheelchair. He, quickly, addresses himself as a a handicap, looking for help.
He politely asks, "I need 50 cents for a bus fair."
"Sorry I'm using a credit card", she responds. Not being aware of the intricate character of the beggar, she tries to be good and polite. After looking at her for a moment, "Right now, I can put 50 dollar in your pocket, if you give me 50 cents", he says. She gets perplexed with the strange offer.
"Wow, good deal, but how?" she asks.
Beating his chest, with his fist softly, "I've the Ghosts power", he says.
"The good or the evil", she asks.
"Both", he responds.
"Both can't stay together, as night and day", she says. Jerry, the Handicap friend and his co-accomplice, he's in line behind the lady. Without being noticed, he pulls a 50 dollar note from his pocket, and puts it on her open bag. "Now check your bag", the Handicap voices. Jenny, searches her bag to find the 50 dollar, instantly.
"It's a magic! I can't believe it", she exclaims in surprise.

To Mikes astonishment, he found Garrison to be not only his work place, but a place where he can associate, with different people and different colors of life. "The womb of a mother's diversity", as they say in East Africa, for him living in the neighborhood, it really became, a place of revelation.

It's 10 o'clock in the night. He's about to leave home. A full moon dim light penetrates the glass window of the store, there he starts to contemplate. From outside he sees a tall young boy,

walking towards him. His name is Dee. With his music I-pod on his hand , in the middle of the street, started to dance. He's just imitating like a rapist. He greets Mike, while still dancing. "How're you Mike" he says, with a big smile.
"I'm fine". Mike responds, feeling little persuading. "Just contemplating my loneliness." He adds.
"Contemplating who?" Dee asks, blinking his big eyes.
Contemplating the lonely moon", Mike says, with a smile.
Dee, chuckles, "The moon never complain for being lonely".
"Get aboard to see what I see," Mike responds.
Again Dee giggles. "You need to smoke the weed, Mike, to see our moon."
Mike chuckles. "Not the real night moon, though".

* * * * * * * * *

I DIDN'T MEAN IT.

Lee, his heart pounding, bursts into the room, where Nicky is sleeping without knocking the door. As she hears the front door open, she stays at her bed just raising her head, looking through the window. In a tip-toe, walks towards her and stands near to her bed.
"Yo! Still sleeping?"
Nicky, removes the sheet that covers her head, wiping her dizzy face, of over sleep.
"Sleeping a nightmare sleep, just lying on my bed, thinking about the weird life of our relationship."

Nicky, since the last incident at the car wash place, she is in a total nightmare, sometime getting out of her mind. She has been sending the wrong signals, almost leading her to depression. In an effort to squash her negative feeling about him, as his eyes turns red, glances at her.
"The issue of yesterday is still under your teeth. If you don't swallow it, it will only remain, like biting a meatless bone."
She turns away her face.
"You're always defensive and I feel that we are not on the same ride.
An uncomfortable silence follows to their discussion. She lies back on her bed and Lee stands straight, two yards apart from her, near the bedroom door.
"You have always time to fight with me, with or without reason. Toothless argument, please stop complaining."
She stares at him in disbelief.
"I'm cursed. God has punished me. I'm hoping where there is no hope."

As she gets up from her bed to make her bed, Lee walks towards the fireplace. With her back to him, to her astonishment, Lee has thrown a couple of one hundred bills, over her bed. Though her mind is fighting, the void future of living in Garrison, as she sees the money, she talks to herself.
"Let the future take care of itself".

INPRISONED IN THE STORE.

Early in the morning, Mike being inside the store, immerses himself into a deep thought, sitting on a chair, floating in his brown work jacket. It has been almost three months, since he has left his hometown.

Organizes his desk, collecting the papers and folders, spread in front of him. Suddenly, his cell phone rings. His Boss's on the other end of line.
"How are things going with you Mike?"
"Things are not proceeding as I'd hoped." Mike responds, suddenly, feeling very innocent.
"Slowly you will get used to it. Though I know the danger of the street. By the way are you scared?" The Boss says, morosely. Again Mike looks down at the desk. He collects the papers and folds them, into their proper folders.
"Yeah! I just feel like I made a big mistake to immigrate to the USA. Here everything functions, but no one lives the real life."

Mike hangs up the phone. Kelly, a prostitute, her soul floating in ecstasy, like flying into the sky, shows up behind the glass windows, standing still. After greeting
Mike, her mind shifts to an idea of sharing her thoughts with Mike.
"Today we're going to rob a bank." She says.
"Which bank?" He asks chuckling.
"Your bank." she responds, glancing at his face, with her tiny eyes.
"One who act, doesn't tell his mother", he says, chuckling.
"I'm serious Mike", she says.
"Seriousness and the drug don't go together." Mike expresses.
"What do you mean, Mike?"
"All your thought's are like our wise father say"... "Without been asked, where you are, responding I'm here".
"What Mike?" She says, asking for further explanation of his say.
"What you need's, the early morning attention." ... "By the way, after you rob my bank, would you give me some money?" He says teasingly.
"Of course". She responds, excitedly. Again, he expresses himself in a saying, "One whom I saw stealing me, I won't trust when giving me."
"You speak philosophy Mike." She says, laughing and pushing herself aside. "I respect your innocence, not the drug you consumed". He repeats.

The Two Streets
MY WAY OR HIS WAY.

Nicky, being inside her bathroom, stands in front of a mirror, brushing her teeth, looking in a mirror. She tilts the mirror towards her face and sees that her hair needs to be done. Taking out, an electric comb and a scissor from the drawer, she starts to do her hair. Looks in a mirror and spends quite time, inside the bathroom, applying some creams and powders to her face.
"This is my best hair done, I ever had."
Runs her fingers through her hair, slowly.
"I'm not kidding! I Hope Lee will not complain. After all I am saving him, from paying to the SALOON."
Coming out from the bathroom grins at herself, stepping slowly towards the sofa, again touching her hair gently.
"Oh, my fabulous hair. Now I feel okay."

Lee drives back home, looking at his face excitedly. At the front mirror, he casts a quick glance around, to make sure no cops are following him. Suddenly, the COP 35 parks behind him at the stop street. The cop steps towards Lee's car and leans towards the door.
"May I see your ID?" The Cop asks.
Lee, slides his hand under his seat and delivers it to the cop.
"By the way, for what reason you are stopping me?"
"For any reason my duty demands." The Cop responds.
After several minutes, the Cop lets him go. Suddenly, Lee moves the drug dollars from his pocket, to the under seat, still watching the cop, through the front mirror.
"My life is looking real adventure. I don't have fun of it. I barely know where my life is heading."

Nicky steps towards the dresser, at the corner of the living room and starts to search, for an appropriate self realizing wear, before Lee comes in. She steps back to where she was sitting, sitting on a sofa. From a drawer, collects a small scissor and trims her nails. After a couple of minutes, Lee reaches Nicky's home. He makes his way, walking down the narrow paved street. Lee steps in through an open door and stands before Nicky, who is watching TV, relaxing and laying on the sofa. Nicky, stays where she is sitting, with her gorgeous long dress stretched on the floor.

In his expression never to ROMANTICIZE it, he greets Nicky, approaching her in unusual way.
"How're you today? The beauty of her mother."
Nicky, takes his say, in a delicate condition, staring at him looking anxious.

"The beauty of your mother! Is that, all your love down payment!"...
"Excuse me, instead of tipping me with sweet words, you made my day hard."
Lee, tries to look polite and good, at the same time looking less worried, about what he said, sitting on the sofa beside her.
"I'm only using, our Garrison expressions."... "You have a strong feeling about my way of greeting you."... "Don't expect me, to say it as Advertised."... "Is not hard, to figure it out. I don't have any Intention, to take an
offense."
She stands straight over his head, gazing at his face, in a bad mood.
"If I were you I wouldn't say it like you said it. Sell it, what is of Garrison, to Garrison. It is very rude expression, I look it my way. I am so much offended."

Lee, gets up from the sofa, again standing straight besides her.
"What makes you so upset? Will you tell me why you are so angry?"
Rolls her eyes, shaking her head impatiently.
"As a female, it is contrary to my notions. Better manage to be honest with yourself, my dear."
He pulls his head back and stares at her.
"I am sorry! Well, I assure you, that it is not from my ill intention, but I see you- you are always the same."
She attempts to walk out towards her bedroom.
"You may be sure of yourself, but I see a difference in your way of reception."
Lee, follows her step, towards her bedroom.
"I am always the same. But, my being with you, diligently and carefully I am calculating it."

LET ME TRY MY LUCK.

After a long week days of hard work, on the weekend, Mike, plans to entertain himself, by going to a gambling store, in downtown. That late evening, as he is inside the store, he sits on a chair, in front of the gambling machine. It's a Valentine day. He orders a beer and a black Lady, dressed in bikini approaches him with a beer on a plate.
"Welcome! A new face and good luck."

He starts to play, sitting on a chair, in one of the Gambling machine. As he tries his luck, he gets anxious and nervous.
"If I get the Jackpot! If I get the Jackpot!" Again more excited, he fixedly looks at the gambling machine, as it's rolling.
"My whole life will be changed. I would say bye, bye to Garrison the cursed street."
Suddenly, King Lee and Nicky show up to the store. Mike is still struggling one after the other, feeding dollars after dollars to the machine.
Lee, rolls his eyes, gazing at the machine.
"Mike! Are you trying your luck by gambling? I am kind surprised."
His gambling attention is stolen by Lee's comment.
"Better than selling drugs, my dear friend. No gun is involved here, besides waiting the luck."

Lee, shows an attitude of a more powerful influential, or better looking.
"I hear you mike, though selling drugs is dangerous, gambling also drains your money." Nicky, interjects her comment, in the middle, glancing and smiling at Mike.
"I know Mike, "One try one luck" but the luck itself has to slap you, to be a millionaire. Never get addicted my brother Mike."
Lee, looks very serious.
"Mike, if you win we will share. Deal or no deal."
Mike, thinking quickly and not showing any hesitation, he nods with his eyes shut.
"Deal! If ever the luck slaps me."

All together in a loud laughter, step out from the store. Lee and Nicky, step towards Lee's car. Lee, before to start the engine, he looks side way at Nicky. She stares at him, with a smile.
"Honey, today's Valentine day", She says. "Happy Valentine day", She adds.

Lee, stares at her face, saying nothing.
"No flower, no nothing", she says, in a whisper tone.
"For me it's just an incredible day", he responds, again gazing at her face. "The day doesn't count in Garrison", he repeats.
"We equally share the influence of the street", she says.
"Love in Garrison doesn't work", he says, chuckling.
"Lee", she shouts, calling by his name, as though she'll convince him about their love situation. Lee, just to avoid their argument, he steps out of his car, and lights his marijuana cigar, already loaded. He returns back to his car, after having a couple of puffs. Nicky's following all his actions, gazes at his face furiously.
"I'm no more feeling you", she says, in a loud voice.

The Two Streets
JOIN MY COMPANY.

It's the last day of school days. It's seven o'clock in the morning. All students, are crisscrossing Liberty Hight road. Little kids accompanied by their parents and the teens, talking with their I-phones, some waiting and some riding the bus. Garrison's clogged with people, and the traffic is high on the streets.
Tim and Jambo, Lee's gang members, are sitting inside a small bar, waiting for Lee to join them. Tim, puts his hand into Jambo's hand.
"King Lee, told me that you are having difficult time to join our neighborhood group."
Jambo, spreads his hands over the table, his heart beating faster. Unconsciously, he tries to drag the glass of vodka, towards him.
"Someone has to save my life, I don't know where it is going to lead me this all."
Jambo, since he is briefed, about the dirty job, of selling the drugs, earlier by King Lee, pulls forward his chair, sipping the glass of vodka.
"I am in trouble, but the one who needs to eat, his mouth gets larger. I am just scared to take this step. It has nothing to do with selling drugs, but personally it's with me."

Tim, hitches his chair forward and sits up straight, pushing away his empty vodka glass, towards the center of the table.
"I feel you, but our boss, king Lee doesn't seem prepared to end the war in Garrison."... "By the way are you scared of death?"
Broad grin of sorrow breaks out across his face.
"Of course, I am scared."... "You know, death is scripted at the time of our conception, and lies on our back, all the way through our life..
Tim, takes a sharp intake of breath. "This's a fucking job!"... "Do you find it this way's normal?"... "Why do I have to do that way?"

That day, early in the evening, Jambo shows up at the store. Jambo extends his greetings to Mike.
Mike, turns his greetings, with a big smile.
"Another day, good to see you, Mike." Jambo says. "Are you alright Mike?" Again Jambo asks.
"I'm alright Jambo."... "I just feel, like I'm in prison cell", Mike says, kind laughing.
"Better, than the big prison house, in down town," Jambo responds, chuckling in his turn.

"Yeah",... "since, it's a cell of my own choice". Mike says.

Kelly, for her part, steps towards the store, as Mike and Jambo are chatting. She joins, their conversations, as Mike's tidying and cleaning the store. "Let me tell you a news", she says, feeling of a mixed feeling of joy and unhappiness.
"Good or bad news?", Mike asks, looking at her face, in the most cheerful spirit.
She gives back her shoulder, looking straight at Jambo, who's standing next to her.
She sighs. "For me it's bad news", she says, blinking her eyes.
"Tell me what's the bad news?" Mike says, feeling quite excited about her situations.
"I'm pregnant of three months", she says, confessing about her life, gasping.
Mike grins. "So, that's good news", he responds.
"To your surprise, they're twins", she says.
"In America, babies grow without anyone's consent", Mike replies. "Not for me, leading irresponsible life" she says, looking ashamed. She's much concerned and paying regard to her prostitute life.
"It's good chance, to change your life", Mike says.
Jambo, in the middle intervenes.
"Once you taste the soup of Garrison, there won't be change", he says.
"I wish, your twins were given, the chance to choose, their mother's womb", Mike concludes.

CONCERNED ABOUT THE UNKNOWN.

Nicky, in her customary wooden chair, is sitting down, facing the window and looking outside over the street, on Liberty Heights. Suddenly, she hears a knock at the front door of her house. It is Lee behind the door, waiting for Nicky to open the door. She steps forward swiftly, taking a far away look, rolling her eyes left and right.
"I was just thinking of you. What a coincidence, I can't believe it. Aren't you supposed to be there in Garrison? This time of the day." She squeezes her hand and both proceed stepping towards her bedroom.
"Did you miss me? Do you think things will work the right way."
He considers all her implications, in light of the reality he knows about their relationship, the blood connection they have.
"Miss you what? I know there is always a price to pay, in any relationship."
She doesn't like the sound of his say. She is very concerned about the unknown and hidden mystery of their relationship.
"Like what?"
Lee, rests his forehead in his hand.
"As far as our relationship is concerned, right now there is no way I can talk to you, out of this."

Though, Nicky feels like a lamb being led to the guild-party slaughter, she's forced not to admit all Lee's actions. The issue of being engaged to a drug dealer, is disturbing her mind. It's a really a struggle between the rambling feet of Lee and her innocent life being part of the street. Nicky, the fact that she can't handle, her issue of rambling with
Lee bombards her mind. As she tries to sit on the sofa, Suddenly, she enters into a deep thought.
"I'm wondering, for all the causes of unforeseen complications."
Follows her stepping towards the living room.

Lee leaves her on her own. He drives his car towards his house. While he is driving his car towards Garrison street, he makes a quick glance at the front mirror. Again glancing out on the right side of the mirror, from behind he hears two police cars, flashing their lights with a siren, coming towards him. Clamping his jaws shut, terrified he watches back as the vehicle pass by, down the Liberty Road.
"These fucking police they are following me everywhere I go."

THE FULL MOON OR THE WEED.

When the sun goes down and the night's to begin, for the majority of the neighborhood, life starts as normal. In itself, practically, the situation's abnormal. The drug sellers and the dealers, they sleep during the day time, and stay awake and busy, when dark. Mike's busy serving customers, when Jambo, approaches the store. He stand outside the store, waiting to hook up with a drug seller, for a refill of the day. Smoking his last stick of marijuana, talks to Mike.
"It really is a horrible thing, to be part of a society, corrupted by drugs."
"Well, are you willing to try new things". Mike responds.
He cloths his eyes and his mouth.
"I have spent all my life on this cursed street, the street I have actually created myself."

From the other side of the street, a young Drug seller is walking down the street of Garrison. Jambo, waves his hand to the drug seller, as he is not far distant from him.

The Drug seller, whistles three times, again waving his both hands on the air.
"Yo, I have only the five and the ten."
Jambo, makes a thumbs up.
The drug seller walks few steps towards him.
After quick transaction, the drug seller disappears from the sce ne.
Jambo, walks back towards the store, to buy wrappers of her choice. On her way out picks her wrapper and at a hiding corner of the store, she loads her cigar, with marijuana.
"If I can't try to reason, through my situation rationally, I try my way through the artificial remedy. I mean smoking my weeds."

Through the open window of the counter, a strong smell of marijuana, rises from the outside the store. The smell is very strong and Mike couldn't stand it. Mike lights air freshener, against the bad odor.
"Mike! Mike! Come out and enjoy with me smoking the weed, a shortcut to the higher mood of mind." He says.
Mike, covers his nose with his hand.
"I am fine where I am! Let me do my job"
Jambo, blinks his eyes.
Puffs another big smoke in a circle.
"You need to smoke marijuana, your dumb day to be bright.

"Marijuana is a power. It makes you think, you can control everything." he adds.

* * * * * * * *

Hiabu Hassebu
BEFORE IT GETS WRONG.

Already the half-full moon is shining, on the eastern part of Baltimore city. Garrison Blvd is quiet and clear. Lee with his friend Tim, is walking and as usual talking about the business in darkness.

Lee, peers over his shoulder, gazing at his face.
"You know we have to break the network of our adversaries, the rival gangs." Tim, looks puzzled, as he scratches his Afro hair.
"How?"
Lee, grabs his hand.
"Before we destroy the whole of their network, we have to cut the head of their leader."
In the middle, they hear the sound of several rounds of gun shots from a distant. People are running away in panic, from Garrison Blvd towards Liberty Road. Jambo is also running towards the store. He leans against one of the trees, shivering as King Lee approaches him.
Lee, taps his shoulder.
"What's going on, Jambo?" Lee, asks.
Jambo, avoids to look at him, turning his back and looking at the street behind.
"I don't know, but I see people running, in panic. I only heard multiple of gun shots."
Both walk down the sidewalk of the street, side by side.
Lee, looks at his face.
"Don't you have a gun? Are you scared. By now you should be used to it. You need to buy a fucking gut."
Jambo, tries to cool down, in an easy mood, despite all of his fears.
"Everything is alright, before it gets wrong." Lee, pauses for seconds, not saying anything. Jambo, raises up his head real slow and scared, his brain ticking in fear.
"I have an urgent problem and I need your help. I can't be part of your association. In my life, I am even scared to kill a fly, let alone to join your crew."
Lee, lights his cigar, leaning towards him.
"Is f***ng too late, you are already in the bus."
Jambo, settles back, wondering where their discussion, is going to lead them, after keeping his mouth shut.
"Don't expect any act of bravery from me, but I will follow the river."

A Rude rival gang member, pulls his car to the BP gas station, to fill his gas. Before he comes out, loads his gun and puts it under

his big black jacket. He approaches the window of the BP gas station, to be served by Mike.
The Rude Gang, gazes sternly at Mike's face.
"Yo! Give me a carton of Newport! You ugly face!"
Mike, returns at his face, a look of a stern look.
"Give me your ID! You handsome face!"
The Rude rival gang, pulls out his gun from his waist.
"This is my ID! Nigger!"
Mike, not feeling fearful, resists not to give him.
"Not scared at all! I was born in war and grew in war!" Jambo, slightly moves towards the Rude Gang, attempting to pull his gun.
"You don't know with whom you are arguing. Mike, as an Xguerilla fighter, never kneels down! Don't you know, where you are standing?"
The Rude Gang, steps backward.
"If I wouldn't trust myself, I wouldn't be here, you nigger!"

Jambo, pulls his gun.
"Backup Nigger! Otherwise, I will blow your head!"

The Rude Gang walks back and retreats the area. Jambo steps forward towards Mike and looking at Mike, he raises his fingers on the air with a V-sign.
Closes his eyes and sighs.
"This's Garrison! Where bullets only reason!"

Hiabu Hassebu
WHERE YOU STAND'S YOURS.

Mike, as he is going to work, on his way he sits on a bench, at the Metro stop in Rogers Ave., waiting for his bus. It is raining heavily and he prefers to sit down, under the Metro station backyard. Gets into a deep thought as he remembers his mother. Picks out his cell phone, dials to his mom.
"How're things going with you, my son."
"Stomping hard, on the street of Garrison." He responds.
"Do you remember mom, what you used to tell me." He adds.
"I don't remember." She says.
You used to tell me."... "Son only where you stand is yours".
But I doubt, if this evil Garrison street, will be mine."
"Don't worry, our Angels will be besides you."

His bus arrives, gets in and sits besides an African American, Old Woman.
"I like your braided hair. Who did it for you? Where do you work?"
"My mom. I work in a Gas station in Garrison street."
"I pray for your safety. Be aware, from this awful street."

Mike, reaches the Gas station store, changes his clothes and wears the work cloth, setting his mind to a previously conserved thought. He looks outside, through the bullet proof window and sees form a distant, Jambo walking towards the store. Glances at him, as he sees a look of panic, in his eye.
"What's the matter with you, Jambo. Did you sleep well? You seem that you were struggling with your bed, all the night."
Jambo, rubs his head.
"The same shit. The same bad nightmare dream. What you expect from this dumb street, besides the drug and the bullets."
Jambo, stares down to the ground.
"Someone might kill me, before I cash my dream. It is Garrison way of life, I can't avoid it, Mike."
Mike's face turns red, out of fear.
"Spit it out of your mouth, for God's sake, my dear Jambo."
Jambo, steps backward and try's to get his breath, violently twisting his shoulders back and force.
"I'm going up, around the corner. Be safe Mike."

A minute later, Mike hears the sound of multiple gunshots, in close vicinity. Jambo is killed by the Rude Gang who was earlier arguing with.

Mike, terrified by the situation, looks outside through the glass window. From a distant, he calls Chief, a young African-American, via a microphone, who's riding his bicycle.
Chief, steps towards Mike and stands speechless, in front of him, shivering, checking his surroundings.
One more time, to make sure of everything, breathing hard and fast, like a man climbing a steep mountain, he addresses to Mike, the killing of Jambo. Out of fear, trembling his whole body, tries to shelter his head, though the incident of the shooting was ten minutes ago.
"Mike".... "Mike", he shouts, looking shocked.
"What happened, Chief?" Mike asks.
"They kill Eugene, Eugene" he, repeats.
"Who's Eugene?" Mike asks, since he knows Jambo, by his nickname, only.
"Your body, Jambo", Chief responds.

CRIME SCENE PLACE.

After five minutes, about 12 police cars and an ambulance, park on Garrison Blvd, cordoning the whole gas station and part of the Street.

Mike has never seen Garrison Blvd to be quiet and deserted. As the police were busy doing their job, one cop approaches him and asks him to let him in to the store. Police, politely stands beside Mike, looking at him with meek eyes.
"Are you the owner?"
"No I'm not."
"Do you have cameras gentleman?"
"Yes we have, if ever it can help."
Mike, leads the police officer towards the camera recorder.
"Here it's."
The police rewinding the video, he starts to watch the whole movement of the area.
"I don't see anything of the incident."

Unluckily the place of the accident is not visible; it is out of the camera sight. The police, turns to Mike and asks him gently.
"Do you know the Victim?"
Mike, feels troubled by the of question in their conversations.
"Yes, I know him as a customer. He was here the last minute, before he got shot." The police, keeps his shoulders up around his ears, as he touches his pistol on his waist.
"Did you hear the shots?"
Mike, nods approvingly.
"Of course, it was only 10 yards, far from me."

I'M HERE FOR YOU.

Grandma in her old age, retiring in her own Villa, just to protect her Grandson, Lee, she struggles all the way, not quite giving up, all her good thoughts. She tries her best, by putting an intense focus on him, to be away from the street. Lee, on his part, the only one, whom he's respectful and afraid of, is his Grandma. But his conscience's full of rage, to kill the killers of his parents.

Grandma, sees Lee's room open and the lights on. She steps, towards Lee's room to see if he's still there. The door makes a whine, when she pushes it. Returns, back to the dining room, sitting on the sofa, blinking hard her eyes, against her tears. Suddenly, her phone rings. Grabs the land-line old style phone. Mike is on the other end.

"Nice to hear from you, the gentle soul from Africa."
Mike, feels ridiculously ineffectual, to tell her about the bad news.
"I'm sorry to disturb you, Grandma. It's hard when things go not the right way."
Grandma, intently follows him without saying anything.
"Only awful things happen in Garrison. I'm used to that just tell me what happened." "One of Lee's friend got shot in my Gas station."
"Very bad news. Right now, I need your help. If it's convenient to meet you in person, possibly sometime next week."
"I feel you grandma and I will do my best to involve myself and be part of it."
She attempts to sit down, before she is to hang up the phone.
"Thank you, Mike, for understanding my pain, see you then, stay blessed."

* * * * * * * * * * *

Exhausted more by her emotions, Grandma, closing her eyes, she enters into a deep thought. She's just praying, for peace of mind from above, to calm her troubled heart. Suddenly, she hears a light knock at her door. It's Lee's childhood friend Mark, who's standing behind the door. Grandma, steps towards the door. As she opens the door, there she sees the unexpected, presence of Lee's churches friend, Mark.
"It's good to see, early in the morning, a beloved soul of our church", she exclaims, excitedly. She, invites him to step inside. Both sit on a sofa, as a smile starts to shine on her face. After

preparing breakfast, she again sits besides him.
"Tell me about the surprise visit?" she asks, keeping her eye on to his face.
"I'm on my way to go to church." he responds.
"How nice for you." she replies.
Mark, without hiding the purpose of his visit, "where's Lee?" he asks.
Looking at him, all over, with her little shiny eyes, she sighs.
"I don't know, might be he's somewhere, around the evil street", she says.
"I miss him a lot", he says.
Grandma, noticing, Mark's sympathetic face, "I know you miss him", she says. "I doubt, if he was drinking, the same Holy water, you're drinking now", she adds, breathing out deep.
Echoing, to her statement, "Lee's quite an honest boy", he says, not to let her be upset, about Lee's situations. "Once, one drink the infected water of Garrison, there's no way, to return back to be good."... "I'm not lucky", she says, sighing. She pauses for quite time, as the house phased into silence.
"He's only a stupid boy, who lost his way, in the evil crowed of Garrison".

Suddenly, Lee enters the house, through the backyard door. He slowly steps inside the house, to see Mark, sitting with his Grandma chatting. Lee, greets both. Grandma, steps towards her bed room, to give them a space to be on their own. Lee, gazes at Mark, with a nostalgic look. He taps, Mark's shoulder gently.
"My old church friend, how's life treating you?" Lee initiates.
"I'm good!" Mark responds.
Both exchange a smile.
"Nice to meet you again", Mark says.
Instantly, both delve to chat about the old memory, as they were going to church, for spiritual and social services. "What drive you, to join the evil street?" Mark, asks, giving him a smile, grabbing his two hands.
Lee, narrows his eyes. "I joined it, just for my own reason".
"For what reason? Mark asks.
"Revenge"...Lee responds.
"Revenge! Who?".
"To kill, my parents killers."
"MY soul will never be at peace, until I drain the blood of the killers", he adds.
"Don't lose your life for nothing, for already dried blood, for a revenge.
"In my mind's still fresh", Lee responds. "I would like you,

turning to a good life", Mark says, highlighting the evil life in Garrison. "It's money, that counts and never found it in the church", Lee responds. Mark, closes his eyes and then opens it. "It's a pity, you stop going to church", he says. In the middle, Grandma, holding two cup of tea steps towards them. She sits in between Lee and Mark. She takes out a long rosary and tries to put on Lees neck. "If ever, the Virgin Marry, would deliver you from all these troubles", she repeats. Mark, as he observes Grandma's holy action, "A brilliant and a holy move, Grandma," he expresses. Lee, on his part confronts her action.
"It'll be a good ornament and I'll wear it, for the fun of it", he says chuckling. Grandma, sighs. "That's not my dream and my expectation", she says, quoting from a Bible verse, "Esau for nothing you labored." Mark, looks deep into Lee's eye. As all their advices, seem fruitless, Mark, one more time intervenes. "If it make sense, I'm here for you, Lee". He says. Lee, again chuckles. "I'm in good shape though", Lee, responds.

BARBER SHOP.

King Lee is following the news of the killing of Jambo, in the local TV of Baltimore city, at the barbershop as stern as he could manage.

The Barber, an African American is sitting on his chair, reading a newspaper. Suddenly, he starts to chat about sport with King Lee, as King Lee is totally immersed, in his own affair. Barber puts down his papers on the table and gazes at King Lee. Holding the scissors in his right hand, gets to his feet stepping towards Lee. The Barber covers his upper body, with a black linen cloth. Brushes and combs Lee's Afro hair.
"The usual style of your haircut King Lee?"
Lee, rolls his eyes.
"You know my style. By the way, am I your last customer?"
The Barber, looking concerned with a nod, touches his forehead lightly.
"There were two customers, with strange faces, here before you came."

Lee, immediately jumps from the seat and steps towards, the video recorder, his hair half done. He starts to rewind the video camera. He pauses, as he sees the strangers, who came at the barber shop, earlier that evening.
"I believe, I have full information, about Jambo's killer. I will get them, before they get me."
The Barber, stares at Lee, distracted by his confusing talks.

That day, the day of Jambo's assassination, people who know him well, being on the street of Garrison, they share, about his honesty and his kindness. Jambo, used to be very social with everyone.

The Two Streets
DO SOMETHING MIKE.

Grandma gets busy inside her villa, cooking and setting the table, before Mike is to visit her. Sitting on a sofa looking tired, tries not to think about her grandson, Lee. All Lees way of life, not to let her down, without knowing precisely of what is going on, she LAUGHS. Suddenly she hears the doorbell ring. She slowly, with her cane walks barefoot towards the door, to open the door. Opens wide her two hands ready to give a hug to mike.
"Welcome my dear, what a blessed day is today, to see the lovely soul from Africa. How are you, Mike?"
"I am fine, just stepping hard... on the street of Garrison."
Leads him towards the dining room. Pulling a chair, she invites him to have a seat, as she steps towards the kitchen.
"You're an honest man, who does his duties. Everyone in our neighborhood are speaking about all your kindness and generosity."
Cleans his face with a cleaning soft, gazing at her.
"A man should keep himself, to be himself, to be a man. Despite my immigrant mind, I am trying my best to act in good way, as far as I can. The merit goes to the womb I was part of, I mean my mom.

After consuming the food both step towards the sofa. Grandma, stands on her feet, her hands shaking.
"I hope you know why I invited you to my home?"
She feels a small twinge of anxiety, down her spine.
"Though I don't talk about it, it is about the weird life of my grandson, Lee."
Mike, returns his attention to her, without speaking a word.
"Nods."
As she is not able to maintain, the degree of engaging with her grandson.
"I wonder, why my grandson, is taking a risk, to ramble around Garrison. How he is going to learn anything? If nobody tells him, when he is making mistakes."
"Things aren't going to change, in this Neighborhood." He says.
"We're living in a hell", she says, in a yelling tone.
"I don't call that kind of life fair. Do you? Mike!", she repeats.
Mike, gives her a tentative smile.
"No, I don't."
She gets furious and aloud.
"Who'll be blamed for all the greed and the foolishness of Garrison?"

She walks slowly along the stairs of the porch, as Mike follows her footstep.
"Will you give me your hand, my kind young boy? If we can save Lee."
Mike, feels less than delighted about Lee's situation as a drug dealer.
"I tried to advice him, many times.".... "But if he says no",... "let the trouble advice him."
She nods, without anything.
"Garrison in itself, is a big school."... "I wish he learns his lesson." He repeats, wondering about Lee's tough character.
She shrugs, looking very embarrassed.
"I'm glad you came, Mike." She says, in low and weak voice.
She sits back, surprised by the extent of his dedication.
Again, Mike sits down next to her.
"I don't know, what to do with myself", she says, looking him in the eye. He smiles at her quickly, before turning his eyes, to his cell phone.
"Are you going to work, Mike?" She asks.
Mike, "Nods".

FUNERAL DAY.

Two of the rival gang members, Jambo's killers, are present at the funeral place. It's lightly raining, as all the funeral attendee, are surrounding the coffin, all wearing black clothes. A middle aged Pastor, steps swiftly, towards an elevated ground to deliver his sermon. The Pastor, starts his sermon, gazing at the funeral attendee right and left.
"Never kill, Never Kill!"... "Only God has to take his possession."... "As for human being, we are not allowed, to take the life, of other people."... "Nevertheless, something has to be done, about this ugly Garrison street."

As the Pastor terminates his sermon, King Lee steps forward to read the last eulogy, the life history of Jambo.

In a raised stage, stands still as a stone, holding the microphone on his right hand.
"Never rest in peace the killers of Jambo."... "The demons will be destroyed, only by demons and mark my word."... "Only one person could accomplish that and get out of it alive."... "Is me, King Lee."... "My decision is final and I am fair enough, to do it."

As he sees the unpleasant killers, his eyes sits on them and pauses his reading, for a couple of seconds. Lee, after a deep breath, he continues reading, pumping his fist high on the air. "An eye is for an eye" as the Old Testament says, soon, so it will be. All feel a sudden sadness looking at his face, not pleased by his say. They get very uneasy and alarmed, for what he said, if he meant it.

All the funeral attendee are silently walking towards the parking lot, all talking in a whisper. King Lee and the Pastor, they meet at the parking lot of the cemetery. The Pastor, expands his gaze at Lee, struggling to keep his voice calm.
"Funerals and weddings, they connect people. By the way, I like your reading, of the eulogy. But-"
Lee, raking him with an irritated gaze, he crosses his arms.
"But what Father?"

To terminate the standoff of words in between them, the Pastor stands and stares at him for a minute, looking at him up and down.
"I didn't like the ending. Aren't you being a bit revengeful."
Lee, glares right back at the Pastor.
"Is not fair, the killers of Jambo, settle in town, with blood in their hand."... "I and Garrison Blvd., we follow the Old Testament."
The Pastor, shoots him a final desperately Unapologetic look.
"You mean follow the rule of revenge?"... "You know that the Old is renewed, by the new.
Lee, smiles and bows to the ground.
"In Garrison we don't reason that way. Revenge! Revenge!"
The Pastor, closes his eyes and takes a deep breath away.
"It's better to stay out of this discussion."

NICKY'S ABDUCTION.

Lee, wakes up from a nightmare dream and senses something is missing. He calls Nicky repeatedly, but there is no answer. He immediately, becomes concerned about her, for not picking up her phone.

Lee tries desperately to reach Nicky. Finally, a Rival Gang answers the call.
"A self claimed king!"… "Your sweetheart Nicky, is under my control."… "We abducted her."… "Unless you show up with our demand, you will receive the dead body, of your sweetheart." He says, yelling.
Lee, snorts so loud jumping from his seat.
"You bitch Nigger! Release her or I will blow your head."
"We will see! Whose bullet, will come out first."
The Rival Gang, tries to make sense of it, in a crackled laughter, rocking back on his heels.
"I've a deal for you! If you give me, a ransom of 100K dollars.
Lee, gets agitated trying to hang up the phone.
"Bitch! You will see! Whether to bake or not, we have to reach the fireplace."
"What do you mean by that?" He says, standing there to figure of what Lee said.
"We will see, whether you get the 100K or 100 of my bullets."
Lee hangs up the phone.

* * * * * * * * *

Nicky's captors, Rival Gang Boss and another Gang, are discussing, about the deal and waiting for the immediate action, of a ransom of 100K dollars, to be paid. Nicky from the inside of a small dark room, her legs and her arms tied, she starts to scream loudly.

The Rival Gang Boss, sits down on a sofa, holding a bottle of vodka and a handkerchief in his right hand.
"The ransom day and place, is finally agreed."… "But know one thing, I don't believe a prostitute and a drug dealer."… Did you get me?"
The Gang, stands above him with one hand on his shoulder.
"I got you as far as the date and the place is set up. The rest leave for us, we will take care of it."

Both, exchanges a special handshake common to the members only.
"It'll be at the barber shop, midnight tomorrow." The Rival Gang Boss, orders.
In the middle of their discussion, a loud scream is heard from the inside of the cell room, where Nicky is staying.

The Rival Gang Boss, steps towards the room, with his pistol on his right hand.
"You better stop screaming....if not you will get it."
"I'm a powerless female, to fall under a wicked gang's hand." Nicky, screams.
He, tries to caresses her breasts and bows down, to give her a kiss.
"You beautiful, ugly creature! Now follow my order!"
Nicky, bows down shaking her upper body, disobeying his order to comply for sex.
"I'm already your victim! But the powerful God, will save me!"

He, attempts to rape her, as Nicky cries loud screaming.

* * * * * * * * * * * *

Lee knows that he must act immediately, to save his sister, as he can no longer bear, the situation. Picks his cellphone and dials to the rival gang boss. Feels a small spark of hope, flaring in his chest.
"Finally I am forced to accept the deal to pay the ransom you are asking."
The Rival Gang Boss, looks at his cell phone, with great happiness, with the eyes of a man.
"You better do it if you want to save your sweetheart."
"Okay, I will put the money at the Barbershop today and come to pick it up."

Hangs up his cell phone. In seconds, his phone beeps again. Tim's on the other end.
"Here it's", Lee says breathing deep.
"Here what?" Tim asks.
"The fruit of the street". Lee responds.
"You know that Nicky's abducted by our rivals?"
Tim, says nothing for seconds. "We've to kick out our rivals, from the neighborhood." Lee, says yelling.
"Right now I'm getting nervous, I can't express myself". "Let's meet in person at the Restaurant", he says before to hang-up his phone.

Half an hour later, Lee and Tim meet at the restaurant. Both corner themselves, sitting in the dark place. They discuss about the Rival ransom money and how to rescue Nicky, in a very well planned strategy, without any risk. Lee shares his plan with Tim, expecting a feedback, on how to accomplish the strategy. Lee, feeling most comfortable, he starts to share his secret strategy.
"Here is my plan!"… "An hour before the deadline, of the ransom day, you're going to stay, at the barber shop, as a customer. Lee, pushes his dish away, feeling, a powerful sense of a rage and anger.
"Hide your gun, under your pants.
Since the mediator is the barber, don't show any sign, besides being only a customer."… "Is that clear?"
"Perfectly clear! It sounds good! Tim responds.

Lee, tugs at the lobe of his right ear.
"As they enter to pick the money, don't act or interact. Just follow their movements."
"Our goal is, not to kill them right away, but to follow them, to their destination." Lee concludes.
Tim, "Nods."
Lee, smiles rather vaguely, advising him to be clever and persistent enough.
"When they start to walk out, with the money, immediately follow their steps, and come to my car."
Again, Tim "Nods."
"We'll follow them, to their destination."
"Okay, King!"
Tim tells Lee, that he will offer himself, up to Rival Gang, in exchange for Nicky. Lee gives Tim a gun. Immediately grabs the gun.
"I need 50 rounds of bullets."
"We are not going to war! Anyhow here it is!"

THE ACTION ON THE GROUND.

As planned, half an hour before, King Lee and Tim, Park their car, in front of the barber shop. Both smoking marijuana inside the car, they watch through the window, if the rival are there. After few minutes, Tim with a bag of money, steps towards the Barber shop to deliver the RANSOM money to the barber. Before the rival gangs arrive to the place, Tim sits at the chair, for his haircut.

Two of the rival gangs, their face hooded, enter to the barbershop, with guns on their hands. The barber, as he delivers the bag, one of the Gangs, he starts to count the money, sitting down on a sofa. As they get out and step fast, towards their parked car, Tim also follows their steps, to join King Lee, who is waiting, in his car.

Now the chase begins. The gangs are driving fast and King Lee is following them, till they reach to their destination, where Nicky is staying, with her captors. As the gang's car parks in front of the gate, King Lee Parks behind them.

Just in time Lee picks up his handgun from his seat. Before he is to dive for a fight he loads his gun as he still seated. Tim leaves out through the passenger side with his pistol ready. Both take off after the rival gangsters. As they approach close near to the rival gangs, they order them to drop their guns. The two rival gangs drop their guns. King Lee and Tim, each pointing their guns, on their heads; they tell them to lead them to where Nicky is located.

The Rival Gangs boss, as he is surprised by the situation, immediately, takes an action. Takes out his gun and tries to shoot at them. King Lee's bullet, reached at his chest, as he falls down, to the ground.

Still pointing their guns, at the two gangs, they instruct them, to move towards, where Nicky is locked, in a small dark room. Tim unties her hands and legs while Lee is leaning against the door with his pistol ready on his right hand. Ten minutes later, they hear the siren of dozen police cars, heading towards the crime scene area. Lee, "Don't get panicked, just walk normal", he says, facing towards Tim. They reach the car stepping slowly. Lee, hands the cars key to Tim, to be on the wheel.

Lee, sits next to her on the back seat.

"How did you see the rescue of the spectacle of your abduction?"
Nicky, feeling dizzy, she sits straight and wipes her face, with her hand, her heart beating faster.
"Oh my god! For me you are like a real hero."... " I can't find words to express for what you did and all your sacrifices."...
"Thank you very much for saving my life."... "It was turning to be awful and bad, but you turned it
good."... "I wonder how you did it."
Lee, stares implacably at her.
She, sits straight and gazes at Lee.
"You know Lee, you really don't see, the suffering I swallow every day, rambling with you on the street of Garrison."
Again, looks at him in the eye.
"It's just... a risk I can't afford to face right now."
Lee, lick his lips.
"Could we...talk about this some more? When I have more time?"

* * * * * * * * *

A bright and a clear Sunday of mid-Summer, Nicky, after she ate her breakfast and fed her cat, puts all her dress, to go to down town, in Baltimore city. As she's, quietly, stepping on the compound of the Habesha Restaurant, she sees her friend Meza coming out through the door entrance. A choking sound from the other direction, rings into her ears. Nicky, steps fast towards her. Meza, without greeting her, she stands in front of her. Nicky, gets so upset and angry, looking at her face.
"You're hanging up, with a drug dealer, just for the sake of money", Meza says.
"I don't give dumb shit, for all your gossips", responds
Nicky. "Listen, how in the world, you speak badly, about me",
She adds. Meza, not taking a notice of what she's arguing about, chuckles and responds, "Did you dream?"
Nicky, feeling furious, sighs, "it's a fact less, no need to dream about it", she says.
"Is your case, a case of an appeal", Meza, responds, chuckling.
"Yes, but not involving the police", she says, belittling,
Meza's sentence.
"I can't digest you bear lies, either", Meza, angrily responds.
Nicky, rebounds with a loud laughter, "You can't speak well, with your trouble making tongue." As, Meza, made her way stepping down the paved street, Nicky, carefully follows her

steps, stepping towards, the Habesha Restaurant main entrance.

Nicky steps, towards the Restaurant feeling a feeling of confusion. As she gets in, she frowns at the door, looking back. Mike's, entertaining with a cold beer, sitting inside the restaurant. She approaches Mike from behind as he's minding reading a newspaper. She politely leans against his chair. Mike, looks back at her, his upper body, half covered by the news paper. "Welcome", he says, suddenly to see on her face, sadness. She gets silent for seconds, gazing at his face. "What happened", Mike asks. "A weird girl friend, just bust on me, without any reason." She responds.
"Never again to fight with her", she repeats. Mike, clears his throat, sipping his beer. Mike, orders, the special HABESHA dish of variety food. Mike, again sees on her face, smiling lightly, to cool her anger. "Do you have unclosed account of quarrel, with your friend?", he asks. "She's a liar and blackmailing creature", She says, in high voice. Spots of saliva, curls at the edge of her mouth. "I didn't expect her, to rain me all the gossip stuff". Mike, sighs lightly. "She's a weird female, betrayed by her hair braider", she adds, chuckling. After, they consume the special dish, Nicky jumps her thoughts, talking about Lee's new drug deal affair.
"I just feel like I made this huge mistake, to follow Lee, rambling around this dumb street of Garrison. I never imagined anything like this."
Mike, keeps his eyes on her, as his hands in his pocket.
"I'm sorry to hear that! Though, Lee is not a bad person, the street that he is stepping on, wouldn't let him do so."
Nicky, pushes her hair back from her head and closes her eyes, like she relishes the feel.
"All those years I have been waiting, for Lee to get me and understand my feelings."
"What good do you expect from this awful street. With Lee it's very hard, to be the middle man." Mike responds.

The Two Streets
THE 44 GANGS AGAINST 66.

King Lee and several of his GANG MEMBERS, stake out an abandoned lot, where they are expecting, a large shipment of drugs. When the shipment arrives, the RIVAL GANG ambushes them.

Two cars of the WHITE SHIRT 66 gang members are seen speeding along Garrison street when suddenly they stop at an abandoned Garage lot, parking behind the garage.

In between a shootout begins with the Rival Gangs, in which one of Lee's Gang gets shot. Lee throws himself on top of the wounded with his gun aiming at the rival gangs. He staggers back bouncing hard against an electric pole. Using the electric pole as a cover he shoots towards the rival gangs, wounding one of the rival gangs.

Lee gets too busy shooting to fend off his gangs as all are furiously fighting in gun exchange. Once they see the rival gangs are retreating the area, Lee with all his gangs, runs out of the scene. Ten minutes later the cops come.

In the middle of the night, Lee shows up, at Mike's apartment seeking for a shelter. He knows, he cannot go back to his home, because the police and the Rival Gang's men, are searching for him.

Mike, confronts Lee, about his involvement, to this dangerous lifestyle, with a fearful look on his face.
"What happened this time, coming in the middle of the night? There is no reason just to disturb me. I wouldn't call it living, I hope you are not expecting the worst."
Lee, gazes at him in a profoundly uncomfortable look. "I'm in trouble! The police are following me."
Mike, desperately tries to calm the situation, putting one hand on the door handle, with a thin smile.
"Don't you know! You are hurting yourself, and the whole of your family? Do you know the damage you can cause to yourself?"
Lee, pauses to catch his breath.
"I am just helping them, by earning money, to support them."
Mike, engages his eyes glancing straight on his face.
"You mean the dirty money from the streets of Garrison Boulevard."

Both take deep breaths at the same time, as Lee begins to read his situation in a steady voice.
"Yeah, but I am caught, in between two goods! I mean that of being a normal person and the dirty money, of Garrison!"
Both smile at each other.
"You don't climb two trees, because you have two legs! I mean, you can't acquire two goods, as you plan for one!"
"I hear you my good friend! I better listen to a wise person, rather than to use my old reasons."

* * * * * * * * * * * *

The rival Boss Gang of the Black Shirt 66, plans to invade King Lee's quarter, in darkness. At that moment King Lee is alone with two other of his gang members playing cards in a dim light. Suddenly, the Rival gang Boss with other six of his members, all with their gun loaded approach the building through the main gate, breaking the lock with a bullet. King Lee's Gang One, jumps from his seat, with his pistol in his hand, stepping towards the door. Gang One, looks through the door hole opening to see the surrounding. "We are surrounded by our enemy the rival gangs."

The rival Gangs, are well barricade around the building, ready with their guns.

Lee steps towards the main door as Gang One, follows him to the door.
"Don't go outside let them enter inside."

Lee, switches off, all the light from inside, as all his members get ready to take their positions. Suddenly, a shootout begins in and outside, on the compound. Three Rival Gangs are wounded and are lying on the ground groaning. One of Lee's Gang is also lightly wounded.

Meanwhile, the police begin to investigate, the surge in gang violence, on Garrison Boulevard. They learn, that the crimes are linked, to King Lee's WHITE SHIRT GANGS and the rival BLACK SHIRT GANGS.

QUIT GARRISON! PERIOD.

After the Gangs shootout, Mike and Lee are sitting on a tall chair, inside at a bar in downtown. Both sit in front of the counter. A tall Male Bartender, is serving to both, as the area becomes noisy and loud. Mike, gets very preoccupied, about Lee's life as a drug lord.
"You call this is a life? Just look at what is going on, in Garrison, the law being handled, by individuals who own a gun." Mike says. Pauses in hopes of an answer from Lee, but Lee is not disposed, to make any.
Both are sipping their beers, in a relaxed mood.
"I wish you slightly, to think about it. You have gone too long with it. Once and for all you have to quit Garrison. Period!" Mike adds.

Suddenly, Nicky coming in from outside, steps towards Mike. Lee, leaves them on their own, stepping down the long stairs. In the middle, Lee looking at himself ruefully, gazes towards the stairs. Suddenly, meets Tim in the middle as he is stepping upward.
"King Lee you seem different today." Tim, expresses.
"In what sense?" Lee asks.
"I see you, very rare in Garrison."
"I'm in no shape to think about my life in Garrison. I think I might quit rambling around here."
Lee and Tim step down the stairs, both walking towards Garrison.

Mike and Nicky step out of the bar.
"I feel like as if I don't matter to Lee. I mean, I never meant anything to him. I am out of this show. I don't feel to be part of it."
"All I do is wasting my precious days and years, that I can't recover them back."
Mike, leans closer to Nicky, glancing at her, mildly smiling.
"Try not to take it so hard."... "I just wish things were different."... "I'll bet you in your mind, you are reading the old one."
"Garrison trained him to be tough."... "It's his business, but I never entertained love with King Lee."... "I doubt how safe it is, to ramble around, with that shitty of selling drugs."

Mike and Nicky, walk slowly on paved path, in Garrison.
"King Lee, has to stop this awful life in Garrison.

Period."
"I hope he listens to my advise."
"By the way, back home in Africa, do you guys consume drugs."
"Not at all, we only smoke cigarette."

* * * * * * * * * * * *

Later in the day, Lee driving his car parks at pumps of the Gas station. Mike, sees Lee through the glass window and waves his hand. Via microphone he calls Lee, who is trying to pump gas at the gas station. Mike, steps out and walks, towards Lee's car. Lee, taps Mike's shoulder, from behind, as Mike attempts to enter the car.

Mike, backtracks and stands in the doorway, appearing to give him an advice to consider his proposal.
"Nothing else to be done, in this cursed street."... "For so long, you trusted the street."... "Always, the same thing and nothing good comes out of it."... "Invading the poor street, day and night, without being secure." Lee, just squeezes his hands, saying nothing, reciting in his mind, all moments of his rambling on the street of Garrison.
"I've an alternative solution if ever you accept it. How about both fly to Keren town, for a vacation."
"I'm contemplating to figure out, if the future holds, anything good for me."... "But Mike, are you sure, you want to do this for me?"
"Sure." Mike responds.
The gaze of his eyes fixed towards Mike's eyes.
"Though it is contrary to my notion of leaving Garrison, I believe, I have to manage it, following your good advice."
"At least you stay away from the Ghost street."

Lee, considers the advice of Mike, to go to Africa. Still in his mind, looming in his thought process, he decides to take that direction.
"If there is anything, I'm up for, at this stage in my life, I choose the unknown, for whatever challenge I may face."

Before Lee, is to leave for Africa, he puts a large sum of cash, in a brown envelope. He sits down on a chair and writes a note to Nicky, to protect the drug deal money.

Hands the bag to Nicky.
"Okay! Here is the deal! Protect all the money, I give to you, till I return, from Africa. Just avoid, the evil street

of Garrison and you can do it."
Nicky, with an angry look her fingers trembling, glances back at him.
"I can consider to be trust full, to protect your money, though, I don't agree to the condition of our relationship. I mean the condition of no love and no nothing."

She pauses for seconds, as if still chewing his idea, over and over, setting her gaze onto his face, she receives the money from him.

Outside at the Dunkin' Donuts place, Tim and Bob sitting in a wooden chair, are chatting and having their late morning coffee. They get concerned, when they learn the sudden disappearance of King Lee, from Garrison Blvd.
Bob, stirs his coffee, staring at Tim in a sad face.
"What happened, to our friend King Lee. Long time, since I didn't see him."

Tim, stares down to the ground, holding his coffee mug with his left hand, turning back his stare.
"Maybe he has chosen the other card, I mean that of returning to the true life."
"Playing with the dirty drug money, the devil's game, didn't work for him. Garrison street, is even tired of him."

Hiabu Hassebu
TRIP TO THE UNKNOWN LAND.

Mike and Lee sit together as they enter the plane. As the plane takes, the highest level of its routes, they start to chat, about the charming city of Keren and the street where Mike grew up.

Mike browses on his laptop and goggles, the town of Keren, showing Lee the different sites and landscapes. Lee, stretches both his hands up, widely smiling.
"Wow! My intentions of changing my life, already started right now. I am over excited, Mike. I will try my best, to discipline myself."
"In Keren town, there are no drugs, no weeds and no undisciplined guns."
The plane lands at Asmara International Airport. Mike and Lee both walk on the tarmac leading to the waiting buildings.
"Am I allowed to smoke cigarette Mike."
"Sure! But not the awful weed."
"I'm not. But I'm struggling enough not to."

On their way before they are to reach Keren town at the suburb they see a camel market. Suddenly Lee asks mike to stop the car.
"What is that and what are they doing?"
"It's camels market."
Lee, sees thousands of people gathered in the camels market place.
"Wow! I have never seen, a single camel, in my life, besides on the American TV. By the way, is there an animal right, in Africa?"
Mike, smiles at Lee.
"Not that I know, but our animals, have only the right to eat and serve."

Lee and Mike, drive towards down town. Parking the car besides a street, both walk towards a famous Tea shop, of Ajak.
"Welcome home. Who is the one beside you?"
"He is my buddy from America."
"Never tell me, that he is a Habesha."
As they are waiting for the special food, Lee smiles at Mike.
"Mike, I am very lucky to be here. Everything is cool and calm. I really am having a fun."
Mike, just comparing the American settled life of a routine and the African way of spontaneity he exclaims.
"Do you miss the Hamburger Lee?"
"Not really? Mike."
"Here everything is fresh, no food conservation."

"I see, "In America everything functions but no one really enjoy a true life"."

Delighted, at the reception of the owner, both wait for the unknown African food, of SHEHANFUL.
At last he is left, to the comfort of eating, the favorite dish of Mike's order.
"Wow! Delicious, I like it. I love it."
"You are here! Enjoy it."

Nicky, before she is to go to Grandma, cleans and tides the house. After she finishes, lies down on a Sofa. Suddenly, her phone rings several times, it's Lee on the other end of the line.
"How's Africa treating you, darling?"
"So far so good. How is grandma doing?"
"She's not feeling well. I'm about to go and visit her."
"I feel guilty, for all those years, rambling on the street of Garrison. I also feel sad about Grandma's illness."
"I hope you come soon."

The next day, Mike and Lee, walk to a village school of SHINARA. As they are near to the village, from far they see, young BILEN girls, washing their clothes, near a natural water fountain. After a long walk, both being tired and thirsty, they step towards the girls.
Mike greets all, using a local salutation.
"SELAMAT" (to mean Hi).
The girls notice, that mike is a local person. He greets them in a local language, with a happy face.
"SALAMAT"
They all smilingly in one voice, they responded.
"SELAMAT".

When they observe Lee, not expressing in the local language, they conclude that Lee is a stranger, somewhat from America. Some girls half naked are washing their clothes, at the water fountain. The girls approach Lee, while he backs backward.
"Hey Mike! I'm kind scared. Don't they get scared of being raped? I can't even believe it."
Mike, lowly gets to his feet, stepping towards Lee.
"Take it easy! Right now you are in Africa. In our culture, young girls before they marry, they are allowed to be half naked."

To quench their thirst, both walk towards the natural fountain.

After drinking cold water, from the natural fountain, Lee glances at the girls with a smile.

"Mike, I am trying hard to get this…I mean the reality of the girls half-naked against my brain."

"That's what I love about my culture. You seem so uneasy, by what you observe. Another world! Another place! Wrap them up, so simple and they will fit, right in your mind."

GRANDMA IN THE HOSPITAL.

Two months after he left for Africa, suddenly, Lee's Grandma feels sick. Nicky, takes her to the hospital. Grandma, is lying on a bed and feels weak. Her poor health added to her old age, she is far gone in a decline day by day.

Filled with anguish in her voice, and tears flowing down her cheeks.
"I wonder! If this time I can make it. My mind, is still refusing, the reality."
"I'm kind scared, for what the word of God says, "You are made of earth, and you will return to earth"."
"Have courage Grandma, nothing to fear."

A medical doctor sneaks through the door and steps towards Grandmas bed.
"The fear of feeling, I have is not about me but about Lee, if ever I am lucky to see him before I pass away."
"I feel you Mom, never the threat of death, dominate your mind. Never despair Mom, hope within the process."
"I did my share, but I am not lucky. I feel I have lost, the only one my grandson."

Nicky, softly, in a tiptoe, not to wake her from her sleep, steps towards Grandma's bedroom. She stands on the right side of her bed. The light is dim and Grandma is lying on the bed, with her right hand holding rosary. Grandma, as she turns her head towards the door, sees the Pastor, slowly stepping towards her.
"Welcome Father George!"
The Pastor stands besides her bed, returning back his greetings, sounding cheerful.
"I'm trying to reach you as is my duty as a pastor. How are you feeling these days?"
"I'm still breathing. I really wanted to get off, this weird life."
"By the way, where is Lee?"
"He left for Africa with Mike. I hope Africa will make him straight and right."
Gives her last benediction, steps out through the door.
Nicky, places a flower and a banner of "Get well soon" by her bedside, waiting patiently until she wakes up.
Death is shining over Grandma's face. Her voice is weak and her eyes are already glazed with death.
Nicky, watches a small smile curl on Grandma's small lips.
"Good news Grandma! At last, your prayers, are being answered.

Lee is completely changed, he made his mind, to the good life." Grandma, purses her lips, lightly stretching up her right hand. "Thanks, God! Good for him. As for me that was it, I hope he comes, to get my blessing before I die."

A FAREWEL FOR LEE.

Lee, learns that his grandma is gravely ill. Mike, immediately organizes a get together, for all of his family and the neighborhood friends, to give a farewell to Lee.

All, gather together under a big tree, enjoying the food, the chat, the dance and the coffee celebration. An ELDER MAN (80) walking with his cane, stands in the middle of the get together attendees.

An Elder Man, puts a colorful natural neck place, made of green leaves, flowers and blue and white ribbon, onto the neck of Lee. He forwards his say in local language as Mike translates to Lee.
"We are glad for you being, part of our community!"
A little Baby girl throws her body into Lee's arm.
Lee, kisses the baby holding her up on the air.
"Cute baby."

The Bilen cultural dance is heats up. A young Bilen Dancer Girl, with her long hair, braided in SHELIL style, waves her head right and left. Invites Lee, to dance with her. Lee accepts and dances with her.

While dancing, she says one word in English to Lee, in a whisper tone.
"Good! Good."
"Good. You are beautiful!" Lee says.
Lee sits down and the beautiful Bilen Dancer, sits beside him. Not saying anything for a second, Lee smiles at her. He faces towards Mike and smiles.
"What a culture?"... "A healing culture!"... "The drug lord Lee, cultured by the simplicity, of the Bilen people, to be a good citizen."
"I'm glad you enjoyed it. I'm proud to have served you."
Mike stands up and concludes the farewell for Lee, speaking in a local language, as all are listening his brief speech.
Mike, looks around left and right with a smile.
"I believe in you, my origin and my people."... "I am proud of my culture, especially as it became, a healing place for
my best friend Lee."
"For a reason of an emergency, tomorrow me and Lee, we are flying back to the USA."
Lee, solemnly bowing down to all, he extends a handshake, one by one.
"Thank you for everything! I will come back! I will never

forget, the gentle and beautiful, Bilen people."
All, clap their hand, as the women shout, a shout of joy.
Early in the morning of the departure day, the secret lover of Lee, the Bilen dancer meets Lee, one more time before he is to leave. Lee is getting ready with all his stuff. She secretly steps towards his room.

Embraces Lee, hugging and kissing him, tears of joy filling her eyes. Despite the language barrier she interacts in a mimic act expressing her love to Lee. Lee on his part interacts in mimic act, as he forwards his last word, by putting his right hand on his mouth and kissing it.
"Bye bye I will see you soon."
She sneaks out through the door, suddenly, to meet Mike standing on the stairs. Mike smiles at her without saying any thing. Steps towards Lee's room.
"Did she steal your mind? Lee."
"No word to express Mike. She is so beautiful creature."
"I wish you were a single, I would have hooked you with her."
"Are you kidding? Mike. How do you know I'm not single?"
"Aren't you engaged in love with Nicky? I don't want any of my family member to be a boyfriend stealer."
"Mike, I'm not so sure how to tell you about the fact of my engagement with Nicky."
Mike turns of his conversation and walks out.

FLYING BACK HOME.

Mike and Lee sit together, inside the plane. Both start to share their experience, in Keren town. Lee takes out some photo and enjoys viewing them.
Mike sneezes, Lee suddenly wakes up, from his sleep.
Lee, feels dizzy of over sleep and wipes his face with a soft paper.
"Huh...Mike, I was dreaming about the young Bilen, half naked girls. They were running after me, as I run fast on the street."
Mike, laughs in a low voice.
"It sounds like you are still swimming to that reality. I hope your mind sets settled."

The plane lands at BWI Airport. Lee and Mike they drive from the airport directly proceeding towards the hospital. As they reach the hospital, they park their car at the parking lot. Both walk fast rushing towards the hospital. Lee, feels himself, completely taken by the situation, of his Grandma grave illness.
"I'm saddened, by the sudden sickness, of my Grandma. Maybe my bad life, is the cause for her illness."
Mike, holds both of Lee's hands tightly.
"It is a life. Never despair, but gather your strength, to sustain it with faith."
Lee, looks very embarrassed about his Grandma's illness.
"I wish I will reach her, before she dies."

Nicky is sitting at the waiting room lobby. Mike and Lee step through the main door of the department. She sees, Lee walking with Mike towards her. Immediately, steps few yards forward to meet them. They meet, at the department main gate. Nicky hugs and kisses Lee and Mike.
"Lee my sweetheart, you just came on time. Grandma is still breathing and alive."
Lee follows Nicky's steps, without any say. Nicky, leads Lee down the corridor, walking slowly towards Grandma's bedroom. She glances at his face with a wide smile.
"You look good, Lee. Africa treated you well."
"After all, eating and drinking, all organic stuff, breathing the uncontaminated fresh air and staying with the natural local Bilen people." Mike intervenes.

Mike silently follows Lee. Behind them, Nicky, walks silently, stepping towards Grandma's room.
Lee, lets out a long sorry sigh.

"Grandma! Grandma!"
Grandma, slightly opens her eyes.
"Oh, my Grandson! I'm sorry, to leave you."
Lee, puts the medal of Mary, the black lady of Mariam Deari, on her neck and kneels down beside her bed.
"You cannot die Grandma!"
"That's not in my hand, but you came in time, to hear my last word."
Nicky joins Lee, kneeling down beside him, tears flowing down from her cheeks.
Lee, holds her hand with his two hands.
"Grandma! Grandma! Don't die."
"I'm not dying, but I am going, to a new place."
Lee, moved by her say he glances at her face.
"You're leaving us alone!"
"Just ready to fly. No one can rip death. As one is born, the death is on his back."

Feeling the last agony breaths shortly, one time opening her eyes, and one time looking fixedly. Both Lee and Nicky, remain kneeling down besides her bed. After a pause of half a minute.
"Do me a favor, one time for your dying Grandma."
Lee and Nicky, stare at her in half smile.
She touches their foreheads, saying her last word.
"I bless you in the name of God. Be strong and faithful. Love each other."
She looks fixedly at Lee.
"No more the evil tendency."
Again, looks at Nicky.
"Be patient! And I am so sorry for not telling you, the truth."
At last, she looks at Mike.
"Thank you, the good soul of Africa."

From under her cushion, she takes out a sealed envelope and hands it to Nicky. Takes her last breath. Her head falls back. She passes away, with her eyes open wide.

THE MYSTERY REVEALED.

Nicky gets busy in the kitchen, walking back and forth to cook food for Mike and Lee. He approaches Nicky, from behind standing beside her.
"I am glad this day to see my life being rescued, by my friend Mike."
Tries, to wash all her hand, with hot water, from the tub. Slightly, turns her face to Lee, in a quick glance and smile.
"I am glad that the rambling feet of Lee, are saved from the dumb street of Garrison."
Thinking about the sins of Garrison street, Lee feels a feeling of guilty.
"I rambled on the street with ignorance, until I learned there was another way out of it."

Mike, on his way drives in silence to Grandma's Villa. Before he reaches Grandma house, he crosses Garrison Blvd. Heads towards Liberty Height, he sees the Church of All Saints, suddenly, makes a sign of the cross. Parks his car on the street and walks up the hill, towards Grandma's villa. Talks to himself in a low voice.
"I am glad to implore the Angels of my country, for the success of Lee, who turned to be good and human." Lee and Nicky, sitting on sofa, in silence are viewing, Lee's photo album, while in Keren Africa. Nicky, raises up from the sofa and steps towards the big framed photo, of keren town.
"May the town and street that saved Lee, be more blessed. I am kind excited what a people! Really beautiful town and beautiful people. I am thankful to all for saving my sweetheart." She picks one photo, from all the photo album, that invited her mind to get curious. Shows, the photo of the beautiful BILEN DANCER, to Lee.
"What a beauty I am kind getting jealous. Who is she and why she is so close to you to the level of kissing you.
Lee, hides his real emotion, to cool down, her emotions.
"She is a Bilen Dancer."

Mike, walks up the hill and reaches near the villa house. Steps in towards the villa and rings the doorbell. He stays still and stand before the door. She hears the bell ring, immediately steps towards Mike, to open the door.
"Is good to see, early in the morning, the face of a beloved one"
"What would be, the surprise of Lee's invitation?"
Walks, through the door.

Nicky, leads him, to the dining room. Lee is sitting and watching TV. Nicky, rushes towards the kitchen, to fetch some food and drinks.
All sit, on a round dining table.
"We lost a great woman of God. A faithful and strong woman, in her beliefs."
"May she rest in peace!
I will miss her company, forever."
Nicky, steps in towards her bedroom. Walks out from her bedroom, with the mysterious letter of Grandma, in her hand. She delivers the sealed envelope to Lee.
"Here you have, a letter from Grandma. Sealed, ready to open it in front of you."

Lee, remembering in distress, all the way he walked alone with Nicky, rambling in Garrison street, ventures to look back, at all his life experience.
"Feel free to open it."
"Not, entitled to open it. The address is in your name."
Opening the envelope, hands the letter to Nicky. She starts to read it in a low voice, in the middle she pauses and glances at Lee in disbelief.
"Nicky! Nicky! Lee's sister! Lee's sister! Are you kidding! Am I in the real world?"
"Yes you are my sister! Yes I'm your brother. I'm serious If you suspect my seriousness, at least trust Grandma."
Mike, is curiously following them, without saying anything. In the middle of their arguments, raises his voice, interjecting to their discussion.
"What's going on with you guys? Anything new to disturb our early morning friendly meeting?" Nicky, gets upset
and tries to walk out, stepping towards the kitchen.
"How come! How come! To hear this crappy bad news."
She touches part of her upper body.
"Is this me? The real me!"
Mike, follows behind her to the kitchen, looking at Lee side way.
"Relax! Relax!"
Lee, feels the room spinning.
"Today is my day to release the secret openly, while you are here as a testimony with us, Mike. I am sorry for keeping it,
for long to myself, I mean, the fact of our relationship."
Nicky, gets angry at Lee and avoids making any reply, crying loudly, cursing and scolding Lee. A flicker of disappointment, crosses Nicky's face.

The Two Streets

"You damn ass! To play with my womb!"
"Don't you know, that the years count on us females? You the lion of Garrison!"
Unable to control the situation, to avoid it, Lee, attempts to step outside the house, as Mike follow him after his footsteps. Mike, approaches Lee from behind and gently he taps his shoulder, as Lee turns his face towards him.
"Guys cool down. Let it be for tomorrow. Maybe either of us will wake up from the right side of our beds, to confront the situation positively."
Lee, gazes to both, moving his eyes left and right.
"If the American Angel can't work, maybe the African one might."
Nicky, leans against Mike, with her hands, curled into fists, shaking her head.
"You better clarify your say. I am tired of the old and I don't know what the new one is or will be."
Lee, sounding shrill about the situation, he shuts his eyes stepping backward.
"A spear thrown and a year gone never return again. Now I leave it all in the hands of Mike. As he rescued me from Garrison, now I beg him to do the same, to clean the mess up of the mysterious act."
Nicky, wonders about his strange say if ever it's true.
"For me it's like "After the rain stops to go to the cave". My young age will never return. I am just concerned about my future."
Lee, gazes at her face, as she is looking for an answer.
"I tell you one thing, "If Lee you trust, leaves you another Lee will come. If ever, Mike accepts it, right now my wish is to hook you with Mike."
"It's Mike who succeeded to get yourself out of it. Though you left me out Mike won't let me down."
"That's all I have to say sister."

At last, Nicky decides not to oppose, Lee's proposal to hang out with Mike. Nicky, after making consideration after consideration, that made her sensible, for a quite long days, she accepts it.

Nicky, leaves the house, driving towards her house. She didn't want to stay the night at Grandma's villa. Gets in her car and before she starts the engine, she looks on the front mirror her face. "I look miserable", she says, trying to brush her hair with a brush. Scarches her car key from her bag and drives in a high speed, down Liberty road. "Once for all I should get over it", She murmurs. Parks right on the street before her house. Rushes towards the house, stepping fast. Jenny, is outside, on the compound taking care of the flowers. Nicky very worried and consumed by sadness, she just passes her without saying anything. She looks her side way, absorbed in a deep thought. "There must be something wrong or misinformation", she says. Jenny, steps in and stands before Nicky, gazing at her face Nicky, remain seated on the sofa. Both feeling free, they proceed with their conversations. Not fully understanding of what's going with Nicky, Jenny, "What's going on with you?" she asks. Nicky, gasps, "I don't want to make another mistake", she responds. "Which mistake? Jenny asks. "No more rumbling on the street", Nicky responds. "Did you reach any positive conclusion? Jenny asks. "I hope soon walking on my foot", Nicky says. She gets surprised about Nicky, change of mind, shocking into silence, retreats to her bed room.

* * * * * * * * * * * *

"You know Mike? All Lee's actions, are like a spilled milk, that one can't recover."
Listens wide-eyed feeling like a stupid.
"I hope you are reading my situation. Garrison street didn't hire me, to be his business partner but his lover."
Mike, stares at her as he sees a bleak of sadness, inside of her.
"You know Nicky, life is made of yes and no; so today's no might be yes tomorrow. For now I advise you to accept the situation as is."
Nicky, red-faced, looks up the roof ceiling.
"All those years wasting my time."
She, stands up straighter, smoothing down her dress.
"In the end to tear apart my life, rambling with Lee, on the evil street of Garrison! Though I am glad that he changed his life, I don't accept all his reasoning of protecting me."
Mike looks puzzled of Nicky's situation. After being quiet, for seconds, he tries to follow the drama where it will end.
She takes a deep breath, straightening her back towards Mike.
"I will talk to you later Mike. Let me close the last episode before I open the new one."

Attempts to walk out the door, with her hand on the doorknob as Mike steps following her out.
"Mike as you took care of Lee, would you mind taking care of me?"

"Don't harness up those feelings of the past. If the horses aren't available the donkeys are ready."
"What do you mean by that Mike? I'm kind confused."
"I mean what you lacked from Lee I am ready to complete it. I mean to be part of your life."
Both hug and kiss, as Nicky's silently weeping and crying.

Hiabu Hassebu
UNEXPECTED VISIT FROM OLD FRIEND.

Lee is sitting on a chair in his room, with the door closed and the shades pulled. In a dim light, before he is to lay down on his bed, turns himself in recollection. Lee's old friend Mark, after he learns that Lee is back home, he pays a visit to Lee. Been aware, of Lee's transformation to a good life, he weakly smiles at Lee.
"Wow! Good God! Nice to see you in this situation, Lee." Lee, touches the corner of his glasses, gazing at Mark, in his mind, remembering the old church's life.
"This will be the day, the Lord wants it. After all this struggle of your life, to see you in this stage for me is a blessing." Mark adds. Lee, looks at Mark inordinately pleased, with himself.
"Thank you bro., for your lovely comforting words." God decided to give me another chance, for the chance I waisted rambling in Garrison street. By the way you are invited for Nicky's wedding. Mark's mouth fall open, astounded, to figure out with hope, if Lee is the groom.
"Good and great! Who may be the groom? Are you the one."
"Not me but Mike."
Mark, again gets more anxious to confirm Lee's surprising response.
"Mike! The Gas station man from Africa! May he and Nicky be bonded in good faith! By the way in my mind, I was thinking you been the groom."
Lee, shuts his eyes, assaulted by a sudden vision of his old life, rambling with Nicky in Garrison street.
"Nicky's my sister. Anyway you are invited for the wedding. See you there, my good friend, the altar boy."

Mark, leaves Lee's house, walking outside, keeping his eyes on the street and his hands in his pocket.

THE WEDDING PLAN.

Lee, turns himself in solitude and recollection, for the sake of helping, Nicky and Mike get married. He gets all serious about the wedding day, marking it on a calendar and listing all wedding attendee names. In his mind, he calls every single person, he could think of, to be invited in the wedding ceremony. It's Sunday morning, a week before the wedding event. Mark and Lee are attending, the mid-day Mass service. After the service, both stay behind and slowly step out, sitting down on the upper level of the stairs, facing towards Liberty Hight street. Mark, somehow distracted, by Lee and Nicky relationship, he asks, "All this time, you were never in love with Nicky?
Lee, chuckles.
"Yes and no".
"What do you mean by that?" again Mark asks.
Lee, again chuckles. "Yes", to love her as my sister and "NO", to marry her.
"Incredible", Mark says, rubbing his head.
"That time I was only minding about my business", Lee repeats.
"How did you see Nicky in your business", he asks, surprisingly.
"As a sole partner only", Lee responds.
"Not really engaged in love?" again Mark asks.
"Not that I know and aware of", Lee responds.

While both are chatting, unexpectedly, in the middle, Lee's phone rings. Lee, steps few yards away, to answer the call. It's Tim his friend calling, from the big prison house in Baltimore. In a collect call. Lee, at first he gets confused, the call being from unknown caller. Lee, picks the call.
"Hello".
"Yo, it's me Tim calling?"... "Long time yo",... "where have you been". Lee, pauses, reflecting and reading his old image in his mind.
"How're you?" Lee responds.
Lee, avoids to chat the old ways of communicating.
"Where're you now?" Lee asks.
"In the big house, yo", Tim responds.
"You mean in jail?" Lee asks.
"Yes, yo".
"I hope you learn your lesson", Lee says, in his mind quoting the disadvantage of living in Garrison neighborhood.
"Do you mind, getting out of the bad way? Lee asks again.
"Is it real, you have abandoned the street of Garrison", Tim asks, suspiciously.

"I regret for the past and I'm new now",... "No more Lee on the street", he says in a kind of whispering voice.
"Do you really changed?", again Tim asks. "Of course", Lee says, loosing no time, in telling him, about the change of life, he got it, while been in Africa.

The Two Streets
THE WEDDING DAY.

The sun is slanting through the big tall trees, making bright strips under the tree shade. As all the invited wedding attendee are sitting on a wooden chair, Lee, sits in between
Mark and the Pastor, tilting his head this way and that way.
"All is taken care of... It is a wedding party... Just excited to celebrate." Lee, trying to make the best of situation, he glances at Mark, smiling with a happy face.
"Mark my friend the altar boy, this time may be the best day, to sing a song in honor of the bride and the groom."
The sound of applause, comes from all the wedding participants, to encourage Mark to sing.
Mark, stands in the middle with his box guitar. After tuning it he starts to sing, first in a low voice then in a high voice in a lyric performance.
All, clap their hands, loudly cheering.
When he finishes singing, all their eyes being on him, Nicky steps towards Mark, just to share her joy and congratulate him.
"My God! You're....wow. What a voice. I am not kidding you are wonderful, you are very talented."

Lee shrugs, trying to look psychologically strong. Old thoughts of Garrison Blvd., comes across his mind.
"This was part of my life rambling on the street."... "It hurts anyway, either to admit it, or to think about it."... "The truth I am facing now, the only kind that matters." He gazes, in a smile, turning his face, to all.
"I don't want to return on the street I grew up. To Garrison, to the street of a war zone."
He, gazes at Mike, with a wide smile.
"I feel grateful for Mike, for being the bridge of my life."

Nicky runs her hands through her hair, getting up from where she is sitting, walks towards Lee.
"My big brother, though I am confused with the old, I accept the new one."
Lee, glances at Nicky briefly.
"My old self-image to be selfish, lousy and rotten is completely changed, thanks to Mike and the hosting street of
Keren Lalai."
He kneels and bows down to her feet.
"Though, I haven't told you the truth of our relationship. On my part I was aware all those years while I was rambling with you, on the street of Garrison."

Nicky takes his hand into hers, without speaking a word, flood of tears comes out of her eyes.
"My relation with you, was only like brother and sister, never lovers."... "We supported each other, trusted each other, though for different reasons, you thinking about me as your boyfriend and I as business partner and real sister."
"I apologize and I beg your pardon, my little sister.
Rubs his head gently, in tears she tries to raise him up.
"I accept, your apology my brother."

All start to enjoy the picnic, with food, drinks and dancing.
Lee being aware of been ill at ease, changes the subject to an atmosphere of joy and celebration.
Lee, stands before all the attendee of the wedding. He gives a brief speech, feeling stable and happy.
"Today is a day of victory, for Lee changing his life, to the good Christian life."
All the attendees clap their hands, as he redirect his attention to the two, Nicky and Mike sitting across him.
"A gorgeous day, for the wedding, of my sister Nicky and my beloved friend Mike. May God bind your relationship like milk and water!"
Lee, after pausing for seconds, looks down to the ground and up to the sky.
"I wish Grandma, is here with us today, to share our joy and happiness."

The Pastor, takes into consideration, the good opportunity, of the gathering of all, standing straight before the groom and the bride.
"Why do you wait, for the wedding ceremony, to take place, in the big Cathedral!"
Taking the matter into his hands, changes his tone completely, with a smile looking left and right.
"Here we're under the trees, isn't that beautiful, if I can wed you, right now."
A short wedding ceremony proceeds.

Lee stares at both of them, as Nicky and Mike are hugging and kissing each other.
"It's the right thing, for both of you, I feel great and happy. I am convinced it will work for both of you."
In the middle of his speech, a heavy rain with frightening lightning and sandstorms starts.
Lee sits down near Mike. The communication is tough, because

of the heavy sound of the Storm.
Stares at the Pastor.
"God be praised, I really liked the surprise! Father."
Looks, at Nicky.
"Congratulation! My dear sister."
Looks, at Mike.
"Good luck to you! My savior and friend! Now my brother-inlaw!"

Nicky and Mike with their umbrella stretched, they start to walk down the paved street. Nicky in her mind reads the mysterious letter of Grandma, silently, all the reading scripted over the umbrella, in a silent scene, read by a professional female reader.

To my lovely grandchildren Lee and Nicky:

> My grandchildren, you know the struggle we went through, all this time. Lee my Grandchild, don't lick, the vomit you vomited, I hope you don't return, to the bad life in Garrison. Convey my greetings to Mike, the real African. Nicky, from now on, accept your brother Lee, as your brother. I wish you all good luck.

Lee, glances back at the Pastor and tilts his head, looking at him straight in the eye.
"I will try to mend my life, collect myself to be a good Christian, with the help of your prayers."
The Pastor begins talking slowly, feeling grateful of Lee's life change and stares off, as if he can see a movie screen, behind him

"As a servant of God, I advise you, never to turn to the evil doings, of Garrison Blvd."
Lee, takes off his black-rimmed glasses and wipes his eyes.
"A vow is a vow! I will do it all through your prayers, Father!"...
"I'll not lick the vomit I Vomit."... "I'll not return to the old bad Habit."

EPILOGUE.

I sit in front of my lap top for a reason. I decided, not to engage my mind, being seated for long hours, to punch the buttons, of Facebook, You-tube and other Entertaining medias. Working in Gas station, for more than a decade, made me reflect, to a reality, as I made it to be, my own reality. The main theme, focuses, first and foremost, on four characters, that of Grandma, Lee the druglord, Nicky his blood sister and Mike the immigrant.

When both parents of Lee and his sister Nicky, were assassinated by unknown mystery killers, Lee's Grandma adopts Nicky to a family in Garrison neighborhood, while keeping Lee at home to be part of her life. Lee was three years old and Nicky one year old, when all it happened. Nicky since she is adopted, to a neighborhood family, has never suspected King Lee to be her blood brother, but her lover. Later in time in their youth age, King Lee knowingly rambles on the street of Garrison with his sister Nicky without revealing the truth of their relationship.

At that time Lee becomes involved in drug selling later to be the drug lord and a leader of a gang group he created. Lee gets acquainted with Mike an immigrant from East Africa who works as a clerk.

Lee, tries to involve Mike, to join his gangs, Mike on his part struggles not to join.
Grandma is not happy with Lee's way of life and attempts in different occasions to confront him and be away from the evil street of Garrison.

Lee, as a drug lord becomes famous and engages with his gangs against another rival gangs. He becomes brave enough to destroy all his rival gangs.

Mike, one more time intervenes, to help Lee, with a suggestion that both of them fly to Keren town in East Africa. Lee not to lose his future as a drug lord, after resisting the advice of Mike for so long, later he gets convinced and depart to Africa.

On his stay in the town of Keren, as he walks on the street, he observes the simplicity and tranquil life, of the locals. Suddenly, his life is changed and he returns to America to reach his dying Grandma who is in the Hospital. Luckily he reaches on time. Grandma before she passes away, she hands to Nicky a letter folded in an envelope, later that revealed the relationship of Lee and Nicky as brother and sister.

Nicky gets upset with Lee, for keeping the secret of their relationship, for so long, but accepts Lee's suggestion to hook her up with Mike.

Nicky and Mike get married at a communal Park.

THE END.